The Treasure of Alpheus Winterborn

John Bellairs

Illustrated by Judith Gwyn Brown

A BANTAM SKYLARK BOOK®
TORONTO • NEW YORK • LONDON • SYDNEY • AUCKLAND

RL5, 008–012

THE TREASURE OF ALPHEUS WINTERBORN

A Bantam Skylark Book / published by arrangement with the author

Bantam Skylark is a Registered Trademark of Bantam Books, Inc. Registered in U.S. Patent & Trademark Office And Elsewhere.

PRINTING HISTORY

Harcourt edition published April 1978

Bantam Skylark edition / September 1980
2nd printing . . . December 1985

ISBN 0-553-15527-X

Published simultaneously in the United States and Canada

Bantam Books are published by Bantam Books, Inc. Its trademark, consisting of the words "Bantam Books" and the portrayal of a rooster, is Registered in U.S. Patent and Trademark Office and in other countries. Marca Registrada. Bantam Books, Inc., 666 Fifth Avenue, New York, New York 10103.

PRINTED IN THE UNITED STATES OF AMERICA

CW   12 11 10 9 8 7 6 5 4

JOHNNY READ THE STRANGE MESSAGE HE DISCOVERED, WRITTEN BY THE LATE ALPHEUS WINTERBORN. . . .

"I, Alpheus Winterborn, swear that the following is a true statement. On one of my visits to Egypt and the Holy Land, and under highly unusual circumstances, I discovered an object of great antiquity. I returned to America with a part of that object—a part that, I daresay, is quite valuable, worth many thousands of dollars.

"I have hidden the object I found, but I have left clues that, when read properly, will lead to its discovery. The person who finds this message is well on his way to finding the treasure. Here, then, is the first clue. It is a poem written by myself and titled 'Mirror, Mirror.'

> "Acorns up
> And windows over
> That will put you
> In the clover.
>
> "How high is up?
> The top of the roof.
> Mind the prancing and the pawing
> Of each little hoof.

"Good hunting. Alpheus T. Winterborn."

THE TREASURE OF ALPHEUS WINTERBORN

"A brisk, full-bodied mystery filled with tantalizing clues and bits of humor."   —*Booklist*

"Bellairs drops clues and plants obstacles tidily enough to give mystery fans a run for their money."—*Kirkus Reviews*

"John Bellairs has a knack for concocting bizarre plots within the framework of the commonplace. . . . Hugo is the perfect villain, from his sinister name to his icy stare, and Miss Eells and Anthony are likable good guys."
                                        —*School Library Journal*

For KEETAH,
who liked it when others didn't

The
Treasure
of
Alpheus
Winterborn

IT WAS a windy night in March. Anthony Monday lay in his bed listening to his heart beat. He was lying on his left side, and the muffled thudding sounded as if it were coming from down inside the mattress. Anthony was scared, but not of the dark. He was scared of what he was listening to. Downstairs, his mother and father were arguing. As usual, they were arguing about money.

"I don't care what you say, Howard. There just isn't enough money coming in, and that's all there is to it. The bills just keep piling up, and I ask myself, 'How are we going to pay them?' How are we going to, Howard? You tell me how!"

"Oh, come on, Ginny. It's not as bad as all that. Why—"

"Not so bad, is it! Not so bad! Well, let me tell you . . ."

And on it went. Mrs. Monday had a thing about money. There was never enough of it around to suit her. She worried so much about money because when she was a little girl, a terrible thing happened to her family. Her father had invested in some stocks that turned out to be fakes, and he lost nearly everything he had. Mrs. Monday had grown up poor, and now she couldn't convince herself that she was well off. The memory of her father's financial disaster haunted her and made her fret and stew about money when there was no reason to worry at all.

Listening to his parents argue made Anthony feel sick to his stomach. He lay there, eyes wide, staring at the dark wall next to his bed. He heard his mother say that if they didn't watch out, they'd all be out in the street. In his mind's eye, Anthony saw his mother and himself standing in the street outside the blackened ruins of their house—this vision always came to him whenever his mother talked that way. It hovered before his eyes like a picture on a movie screen. He wondered if his family really would go broke someday. He worried a lot about money, and considering what his mother was like, this was not very surprising.

Finally, the argument was over. Anthony heard his mother's chair scrape back as she got up and started fixing Mr. Monday's supper. It was almost midnight. Mr. Monday worked late six nights a week. He ran a saloon. In the town where the Mondays lived, nice people didn't run saloons, and the Mondays tried hard to be nice people, so they called their saloon a cigar store: Monday's Cigar Store. And there actually were some dusty glass cases up in the front of the store that

4

had cigars in them. Mostly, though, Monday's Cigar Store sold beer and wine by the glass. Running the place was hard work, and Mr. Monday ran his saloon all by himself. He had hired a helper once, but Mrs. Monday had accused the helper of stealing money out of the cash register, so Mr. Monday had let him go. Anthony often wished he were old enough to help his dad out, but state law said you had to be eighteen to work in a place where liquor was sold, and that was that. Anthony's brother, Keith, who was sixteen, would be able to help their father in two more years. But for now, Mr. Monday had to go it alone.

It was silent downstairs now, except for the sound of bacon sizzling. Anthony rolled over and tried to sleep. Wild shadows, cast by the swinging street lamp on the corner, leaped across the bedroom wall. From across the hall, Anthony could hear the sound of his brother's snoring. Keith was lucky. He could sleep through anything. Meanwhile, Anthony lay awake, worrying. He worried about what would happen if his dad got so sick that he couldn't work. There wasn't much work that a thirteen-year-old boy could do. He could get a paper route, but you hardly made anything at all doing that. . . .

The shelf clock downstairs struck half past twelve. Anthony started to feel drowsy, and as always, his mind drifted from worry into daydream. First he was a diver, stumping across the floor of the ocean in a diving suit, poking among the rotting ribs of a Spanish galleon till he found a chest full of gold coins. Then he imagined himself sitting at his own kitchen table downstairs. The table was covered with a heap of gold coins. Behind him stood his parents. They were smiling as they looked at the glittering mound of wealth. Now his mother would never have to worry about money again, not ever. . . .

5

And with this pleasant image before his eyes, Anthony fell asleep.

The next day after school, Anthony decided to stop by the library on his way home. He did this a lot, not so much because he was a bookworm, but because he liked the librarian, Miss Eells. Miss Myra Eells was the librarian at the public library in the town of Hoosac, Minnesota, where Anthony lived. Anthony had met her one day when the two of them were browsing at the same magazine rack in a drugstore. They had gotten into a conversation, and after that they had gotten to be friends. Anthony liked Miss Eells. In many ways, she was closer to him than his own mother was. For one thing, he wasn't scared of Miss Eells. He felt comfortable with her. It wasn't the same way with his mother. She always seemed to be bawling him out or telling him that he was worthless and stupid and selfish.

But with Miss Eells it was different. She took Anthony seriously. She listened to him. She took time off from her work to just sit around and be with him, and that meant a lot to Anthony. Miss Eells did other things for him, too. She bought Anthony presents and took him for rides in her car. She had taught him how to play chess, and she had taught him a code that had been used by spies during the Civil War. Anthony and Miss Eells left each other messages in this code because it was fun to do. Sometimes Anthony wondered why she was so nice to him. Anthony didn't have a lot of friends, and he didn't think much of himself—that is, he didn't think he was a very wonderful person—so it was only natural that he would wonder why Miss Eells wanted to be friends with him. Anthony's mother was always telling him to watch out for people who were nice to you because they were

7

only trying to butter you up so they could take advantage. Luckily for Anthony, he didn't always follow his mother's advice. He took Miss Eells's love for what it was and was happy with it.

Whistling cheerfully, Anthony trotted down Minnesota Avenue, the main street of town, and crossed Levee Park. It was a chilly March day, and Anthony was wearing his brown leather jacket and his red leather cap. He had always worn red leather caps, ever since he could remember, and he had always scrunched the peaks on them so they were curved. He was funny about things like that.

When he got to the far side of the park, he stopped and looked up at the library, a dark shape looming over the bare trees. He always stopped and stared at the library before he went into it. Even people who walked along with their noses to the ground would often look up when they passed it. It was really something to stare at.

The Hoosac Public Library was like a castle out of a fairy tale. Of course, it was a bit smaller than most castles, being only two stories high. But it had battlements like a castle, and funny little bulges here and there with narrow loophole windows, the kind that soldiers might shoot through when they saw the enemy coming. At one corner was a tall round tower with a slate roof and a weather vane with a reindeer on it. Like a castle, the building was made of stone, black stone that glistened when it was wet, and it was covered with fantastic carvings. The carvings nestled in all the angles and corners of the building. They showed stone dwarfs hammering on stone anvils, stone scholars reading stone books, stone dragons breathing curls of stone steam, and

8

many other strange things. Over the main doorway of the library was a carving that showed a half-moon. The moon was the kind that you see in Mother Goose books, with a face and a big, long nose:

Under the moon face was a stone banner, and on it these words were carved: BELIEVE ONLY HALF OF WHAT YOU READ.

It was a funny kind of inscription to put over the door of a library. But then, the Hoosac Public Library had been built by a funny kind of man.

The Hoosac Public Library had been designed, built, and paid for back in 1929 by a man named Alpheus T. Winterborn. Mr. Winterborn had been rich—very rich. He had made his money from a company that still employed about half the people in Hoosac—the Winterborn Silverware Company. Winterborn Silverware made silver-plated objects of all kinds—knives, forks, spoons, teapots, percolators, tea strainers and tea balls, and Edam cheese holders—things like that. The company also cast statues in bronze and other metals. In fact, it had cast the small bronze reindeer on the weather vane atop the tower of the library. The company had gotten to be famous nationwide, like the 1847 Rogers Brothers, and it had made Alpheus Winterborn a millionaire.

Millionaires often spend their money in strange ways, but none of them ever spent his more strangely than Alpheus Winterborn did. In the last twenty years of his life, he went from one fad to another. First he decided that he was going to be an inventor. He tried to invent a perpetual-motion machine, a gadget that would run all by itself, without steam or electricity or gasoline or any kind of fuel. He tinkered for years, but all he ever came up with were some funny-looking gadgets that would run for two or three hours and stop. But Alpheus Winterborn wasn't discouraged. He had a lot of money and a lot of time. Next he decided that he would be an archeologist. This was in 1922, when the whole world was talking about King Tut's tomb, which had just been discovered. Alpheus Winterborn didn't see why he couldn't discover something, too, so he bought a pith helmet, a pick, a shovel, and a lot of other gear and went to Egypt. He dug at Luxor, at Karnak, and at some other places on the Upper Nile. Then he went to the Holy Land and did some digging there. When he came back to Hoosac after being away for almost two years, rumors started to fly around. People claimed that old Alpheus had discovered something strange and wonderful, something really valuable. No one knew for sure what the thing was or who it was who had started the rumors, but there were many people in the town of Hoosac who would swear on a stack of Bibles that Alpheus Winterborn had made a find.

Whatever this mysterious treasure was, nobody ever saw it. Alpheus Winterborn remained his usual stolid, uncommunicative self, and after a few months in Hoosac he was off to the Near East again. He made three trips in all to Egypt and Palestine, and every time he returned home, the mysterious rumors started up again. But there are always people in every town who will start rumors, and generally the rumors have no foundation at all.

After his last trip, Alpheus Winterborn came back to Hoosac and shut himself up in his house. He saw no one and talked to no one. He had always been an odd person and the subject of much gossip in the town of Hoosac. But he was odder now than he had ever been, and people began to wonder if maybe they would wake up some morning and find that he had hanged himself from the chandelier in his living room.

Just when public curiosity reached a fever pitch, Alpheus Winterborn came out of hiding. He was nearly seventy, but there was life in the old boy yet. He announced that he would become an architect. What he designed was the Hoosac Public Library. He built it as a kind of shrine to his own memory, just as the Pharaohs of ancient Egypt built their pyramids to house their bodies, their souls, and the record of their accomplishments. On the second floor of the building there was to be an Alpheus Winterborn Reading Room. It was to contain, among other things, a long, windy account, written by himself, of his archeological diggings. No one could figure out why he wanted to leave behind a record of his career as an archeologist, since he had never found anything worth mentioning—except for the mysterious treasure that everyone talked about. But he was a strange man. And because he was rich, he could pretty much do what he pleased.

For the last two years of his life, Alpheus Winterborn was all wrapped up in the library he was building. Day after day he went down to watch the men who were working on it. He would pace back and forth with a roll of blueprints in his hand, carping and making suggestions till the workmen were sick of the sight of him. Finally, though, it was finished in the late fall of 1929. And then Alpheus Winterborn did the strangest thing. The library was to have opened on the first of November, but Alpheus Winterborn ordered that the opening be delayed for a week. Why? Because he wanted to live in the library. To live, as he put it, "inside my own creation," for just seven days.

It was certainly a strange request, but since Alpheus Winterborn was putting up the money for the library, everybody had to do what he wanted. So for a solid week, old Alpheus Winterborn lived in the newly finished Hoosac Library. During that time he never went out. The shades and the drapes on all the windows were pulled tight, but people who passed the library that week thought they could catch glimpses of him going to and fro with a lighted candle in his hand. At the end of the week, he came out and told the mayor and the city council that they could have their grand opening at last. Two weeks later, Alpheus Winterborn was dead.

Anthony stood staring at the library and thinking of all the wild stories he had heard about Alpheus T. Winterborn. He wondered if his mysterious treasure really did exist, and if it did—where? Then he snapped out of his trance and started walking again, and as he walked, he whistled a popular tune that was on the radio a lot. He stopped whistling as soon as he opened the front door of the library because, as he very well knew, you were supposed to be quiet in libraries. He looked around for Miss Eells. Where was she? She wasn't at the main desk, so maybe she was in her office. No, she wasn't there, either. Finally he found her in the West Reading Room. She was standing at the top of a stepladder with a long-handled feather duster in her hand. As she swept the duster back and forth across the faded spines of books, clouds of dust filled the room. Anthony started to call to her, but before he could get anything out, he began to sneeze. Miss Eells stopped dusting and turned around.

12

Miss Eells was a small, birdlike woman with a wild nest of white hair on her head. Everything about Miss Eells was birdlike. Her eyes, behind her gold-rimmed glasses, were small and bright, like the eyes of a bird, and the quick, darting, side-to-side motions of her head were birdlike, too. The bones of her hands were small and delicate, like the bones of a bird. Her voice was quiet and precise, but oddly enough she had a large vocabulary of curse words. She used these words only on special occasions. Anthony especially remembered the time an entire box of Ohio kitchen matches burst into flame in her hand when she was lighting a fire in one of the library fireplaces at Christmastime. He had been the only one in the library with her, and he still remembered how strange it had been to hear her pour forth a stream of profanity in that well-modulated, ladylike voice of hers.

"Well, hello, Anthony! What brings you to the . . . aah . . . the aaaaaAAAAACHOOOO!" Miss Eells sneezed loudly. Anthony sneezed again, too, and then both of them laughed. "I had better open a few windows," she said as she climbed down from the step-ladder. "Otherwise we'll both die of the convulsions."

Anthony followed Miss Eells around the room as she opened the tall windows with transoms at the top. To open the transoms she used a long pole with a hook on the end. Anthony liked to watch her do this. Then Miss Eells went to her office and started making tea.

It took her some time. As Anthony had noticed before, Miss Eells had trouble doing some things, in spite of her brisk, businesslike air. While he sat waiting patiently, she knocked the hot plate halfway off its little table when she tried to turn it on. Finally she got the switch to obey her, and the coil of wire began to glow red. As soon as she had the hot plate set straight on the table, she took a step backward and knocked the teakettle off the corner of her desk. With a sigh, she stooped, picked up the kettle, and carried it into her private bathroom to fill it. Anthony heard the kettle drop into the sink a couple of times, and he heard Miss Eells saying something under her breath.

Now the kettle was warming up on the hot plate. Miss Eells opened a small built-in cupboard in the wall behind her desk and took out two cups, two saucers, and the sugar bowl. She tried to hold them all at once, and she just barely managed to get them all to the desk without dropping them. Then she knocked over the sugar bowl and spent several minutes carefully sweeping the spilled sugar off the desk blotter into the little bowl. Some eraser dust and pencil shavings got mixed in with the sugar, but Miss Eells didn't notice.

By now, Miss Eells was looking flustered and a bit disheveled. She sat down and mopped her face with her pocket handkerchief. "Well now, Anthony! And how is the world treating you these days?"

Anthony frowned. "Not so good, Miss Eells. My folks were arguing again last night. It made me feel real bad."

Miss Eells smiled sympathetically. "Money again?"

"Yeah. My mom thinks that we don't have enough money to live on and that we'll all be out in the street if we don't watch out."

Miss Eells had to bite her tongue to keep from saying that his mother was a worrywart, but of course she couldn't say this, not to Anthony, so she just sat and watched the kettle with a discontented look on her face.

"Miss Eells?"

"Yes, Anthony? What is it?"

"Do you think the man that built this library really did hide a treasure somewhere?"

"Oh, *that* old story! You mean you've heard it, too? Well, who knows if it's true? But I'm afraid the only treasure you and I will ever see, Anthony, is the money we make by working for it."

Anthony said nothing. He just looked gloomy. Miss Eells went back to watching the kettle, but then, quite suddenly, she had an idea. Turning to Anthony, she said, "Do you think you'd be happier if you had a job of some kind?"

Anthony brightened up immediately. "Wow! You bet I would! Do you know about a job I could get?"

"No," said Miss Eells. Anthony's face fell, but she added quickly, "However, and be that as it may, I am the librarian here, and now and then I have a little extra money to play with. And too much work besides. Most people think all a librarian has to do is check out books. How would you like to be a page at this library?"

Anthony was mystified. The only pages he'd ever heard of, aside from the pages in a book, were the little boys in fairy tales who came in and blew horns and announced things. They wore funny-looking costumes and had shoes with long, pointed toes. Anthony wondered if that was the sort of thing Miss Eells had in mind.

Miss Eells smiled. She could tell that Anthony didn't have the faintest idea of what a library page was. She had just opened her mouth to tell him when the kettle started making about-to-boil noises. It trembled and rattled and whined, and little wisps of steam came curling out of the spout. Miss Eells got up and opened the cupboard again. She took out a big brown teapot with a gold band around it, and a yellow box of Lapsang Souchong tea. Then she took the kettle off the hot plate and poured a little of the boiling water into the teapot. She swirled it around and dumped it into a potted geranium in the corner. The geranium was dying, and the hot water wasn't going to help it much. As Miss Eells struggled to get the lid off the tea box, she broke a fingernail, but finally she managed to pry it off. Three spoonfuls went into the pot, and in went the boiling water. They waited for the tea to steep; then Anthony held the strainer as Miss Eells poured it out. It smelled smoky and tasted strange, but Anthony didn't mind. He just liked the idea of having tea with Miss Eells. It was a warm, friendly thing to do.

"Now, then," said Miss Eells as she sipped her tea, "where were we? Oh, yes. A library page has all sorts of duties. He has to take books that have been returned to the library and put them back in their proper places. You'll have to know something about the Dewey decimal system, but that's easy enough to learn. Then you'll have to get books for people, and—"

Anthony looked puzzled. "How come they can't go get them themselves?"

Miss Eells grinned and cocked her head to one side. "Anthony, I know this is hard for you to understand, but most people who come into a library don't have the faintest idea of how to find a book. They don't know how to use the card catalog, and they think the Dewey decimal system is something kids learn in arithmetic class. That's where you come in. You look up the book for them and bring it out to the circulation desk. If you happen to be tending the desk at the time, you stamp the book out for them. Some things, like the back issues of magazines, are kept in a locked room in the basement. If someone wanted one, you would have to go downstairs and get it for them. Then there are all sorts of general tasks, like lighting the fire in the West Reading Room fireplace in the wintertime, and tidying and dusting and

things of that sort. Which brings me to something that I feel I have to tell you. If you take the job, you start tomorrow, and tomorrow is the twenty-first of March. Do you know what the twenty-first of March is?"

"Groundhog Day?"

Miss Eells glared at Anthony over the top of her glasses. "Groundhog Day indeed! Go to the foot of the class, as my late father used to say. It's the vernal equinox, the first day of spring! It is also the day when I start the spring cleaning of the library. Do you think you're ready for that?"

"Gee, I dunno. What do I have to do?"

"Oh, not much. You just have to help me polish the woodwork and clean the floors and dust the bric-a-brac and clean the windows and . . ." Miss Eells stopped talking and burst out laughing when she saw the horrified expression on Anthony's face. "Oh, Anthony, come *on*! I'm just kidding! I will have a *few* extra chores for you to do, but I'm not Simon Legree. You can do what you feel like doing. How about it? Are you interested in the job?"

Anthony grinned and stuck out his hand. "Put 'er there, Miss Eells!" he said.

Miss Eells stuck out her hand, too, and as she did so, she knocked over her cup of tea.

Chapter 2

Hoosac, Minnesota, was on the Mississippi River. It was a long, skinny town, shaped like a cigar, with the Mississippi on one side and a long artificial lake called Lake Hoosac on the other. All around the town the land was as flat as a tabletop, but in the distance, on either side, rose tall bluffs. The bluffs were very tall, six or seven hundred feet high, and they were covered with trees. The bluffs on the western side of the town were a long way away, but the ones on the eastern side were quite close. They seemed to tower over the town: Anthony could see them from his bedroom window. Sometimes before he went to bed, he sat in the window and stared at them as they lay shrouded in darkness or glimmering in the moonlight.

It was funny to think that those bluffs were in

Wisconsin. Watching them from his window, Anthony was in Minnesota. The river was the boundary, and it was other things, too—a sort of liquid highway for all sorts of barges and boats. The river traffic was not as important to the town as it had been in the steamboat days that Mark Twain wrote about, but it still went on. Often during the night, Anthony could hear the horns of the barges hooting. The sound echoed in the hollow iron holds of the vessels. It was a lonely sound, but somehow nice to listen to as you lay in bed at night. Anthony thought that Hoosac was a nice place to live.

When Anthony sat down at the dinner table with his family that evening, he was bursting with good news. His face showed it, and when his mother passed him the peas, she said suspiciously, "Well! What have you been up to, hmmm?"

"I've got a job, Ma!" said Anthony excitedly.

His mother stared at him blankly. "A job? Doing *what*?"

"I'm gonna be a page down at the library. Miss Eells got me the job!"

Mrs. Monday's eyes narrowed. She didn't like Miss Eells much because she was jealous of her. Mrs. Monday often behaved as if she didn't like Anthony, either, but in her strange way she was greatly attached to him, and she resented the idea that somebody else might try to be a mother to him.

"She wants you to work for nothing, I'll bet!" replied Mrs. Monday.

Anthony winced. Then he got angry. "No, she doesn't, Ma!" he shouted. "She's gonna give me a dollar an hour! Whaddaya think of *that*, huh?"

"Mom can hear you, Tony," said Keith, glancing nervously at his mother. "You don't have to yell."

20

"I don't care! She always thinks that Miss Eells is a kook or a crook, and she isn't. She isn't, *she isn't!*" Anthony screamed these last words at the top of his voice.

Mrs. Monday laid down her knife and fork and glared grimly at Anthony. Her voice trembled as she spoke. "Anthony Monday, if you cannot control yourself any better than that, you had better leave the table. Go up to your room at once!"

Anthony got up, shoved his chair back into its place, and walked out of the room. He went upstairs, sat down at his desk, and cried.

Later, when everybody else had finished eating, Anthony came down and ate his cold food. Then he decided that he would go out to the garage to see what his brother was up to. On his way out, he passed through the kitchen, where his mother was washing dishes.

"I'll bet she never pays you," Mrs. Monday said without turning around. Anthony said nothing. He clattered down the back steps and went out to the garage.

Anthony's older brother, Keith, was nuts about cars. When he was little, he used to play endlessly with cars and trucks, and he had really never grown out of it. The side yard of the Mondays' house was strewn with rusting radiators, dented fenders, and other car parts. At present, Keith was working on the family car. The hood was open, and from the ceiling of the garage hung a spotlight on a long cord. Keith was dressed in gray coveralls, and his hands and face were streaked with grease. Wrenches and rags lay draped on the fender. When he heard the side door of the garage open, he looked up and smiled. "Hi, kid! Hey, don't listen to the things that Mom says. She doesn't always know what she's talkin' about! I think it's great that you got a job. When I was your age,

21

I couldn't even get a job as a crummy paper boy. Congratulations!"

Anthony beamed. He liked his brother a lot, and at times like this, he liked him more than he could say. Anthony hung around the garage for an hour, just watching Keith work and talking to him. Then he went in to do his homework. He felt a lot better.

The next day after school, Anthony started his new job. It turned out to be a lot of fun. He liked poking around in the stacks, climbing up on ladders, and fetching down books for people. He felt important when he sat at the main desk and looked around at all the people who were sitting and reading in armchairs or at tables. He even enjoyed answering the weird questions that people asked him over the phone, like "Who were the first three governors of Minnesota?" or "Could you find out for me the real name of the Minnesota novelist Frederick Manfred?" or "Where is the nearest state where you can get married without a blood test?"

Needless to say, Anthony couldn't answer any of these questions off the top of his head. What he did was write them down and take them to Miss Eells, who would then tell him where to look up the answers. (In the case of the blood test, she suggested that Anthony say he didn't know and hang up politely.) In a little while, Anthony got so good at the question-answering game that he could go directly from the phone to the right reference book without having to ask Miss Eells anything.

When he was off duty, or when there was nobody in the library but Miss Eells and him, Anthony would explore. It was a big old building, and only about half of it was really needed, or used, by the library. On the second floor was a little museum run by the Hoosac

Historical Society. It was hardly ever open, but since Anthony had the keys to all the rooms and display cases when he was on duty, he would sometimes pop into the museum and try on Civil War helmets or play with the antique pistols and swords that were exhibited there. He was always very careful to put everything back where he had found it when he was through fooling around.

There were other rooms, too. Some were small and spooky. There was a little auditorium where lectures and slide shows were sometimes put on. There was a smoking room, equipped with easy chairs and ash trays for those who wanted to smoke while they were visiting the library. There was the Alpheus Winterborn Reading Room, a comfy little parlor full of sofas and overstuffed chairs. In this room were glass cases containing models of the perpetual-motion machines that Mr. Winterborn had tried to invent, and in the bookcases that lined the walls were all the books that had been in Alpheus Winterborn's personal library. Some were books on archeology, such as *Interesting Tombs of the XIX Dynasty* or *Monuments of the Fayyum.* Some had to do with architecture, like the works of Vitruvius and Palladio. And of course there was Mr. Winterborn's long and boring account, written out in longhand, of his archeological career.

At one end of the room was a marble fireplace, and over it was a portrait of Alpheus Winterborn in a heavy gilt frame. It showed him as he had been when he was young, in the 1870s, when beards were in fashion. Anthony thought he looked like one of the Smith Brothers on the cough-drop package. He often found himself staring at this portrait. The expression on the man's face interested him. Maybe it was just Anthony's imagination, but it seemed to him that Mr. Winterborn

23

was amused. It was as if he were enjoying some wonderful secret joke, and Anthony couldn't help wondering what it was.

Weeks and months passed. June came, and school let out. Miss Eells asked Anthony if he wanted to keep on working at the library during the summer. He said sure. He was even willing to work longer hours than before. Most of his friends had summer jobs, and Anthony really liked being at the library more than he liked being at home. If he sat around at home doing nothing, his mother found something for him to do, or else she made him feel so guilty that it wasn't any fun sitting around. And of course he liked the money he was being paid. Every Friday he got a little brown envelope with his wages in it. He spent some of the money on movies and popcorn and comic books and things of that sort. The rest he put in the bank. One day Anthony went down to the First National Bank of Hoosac with his father and proudly opened up his own personal savings account. It made him feel good to have a savings account like the one his parents had. He felt that somehow he was contributing more to the family than he had been before. The bankbook made him feel that he was really worth something.

The rest of June passed, and July began with a heat wave. The temperature rose to one hundred and stayed there. Everything was sticky or hot to touch. The pavement burned under the soles of your feet as you walked along, and it took great effort just to move.

On one of these broiling hot days—a Wednesday it was—Anthony was in the West Reading Room, changing the magazines in the magazine rack. All the windows were open, and the curtains on the long windows hung limp. In the corner, a girl in shorts was reading a copy of *Seventeen*, and an old lady was browsing along one shelf. A fly buzzed past Anthony and sailed up toward the ceiling. As Anthony followed it with his eye, he happened to glance at the carvings over the fireplace. He had noticed them before because they were so strange-looking.

There was a wide, square panel covered with three-dimensional carved objects that stood far out from the wall. There were oranges and lemons and sheaves of grain and bunches of grapes and clambering monkeys and, here and there, odd little faces peeping out through the carved shrubbery. At the top of the panel was a pointed cornice; on the point was a half-moon just like the stone half-moon and banner over the front door. On the banner was the same motto: BELIEVE ONLY HALF OF WHAT YOU READ.

As Anthony stood looking up at this wilderness of carved wood, it occurred to him that the panel needed dusting. Big cobwebs festooned the monkeys and grapes and grain, and gray dust lay thick in all the crevices.

Anthony suddenly felt like giving that panel a good, hard dusting. It was a hot day, and his clothes were soaked with sweat, but he didn't care. He felt energetic, and besides, it would be a nice thing to do for Miss Eells. Down to the basement he went. He got out the stepladder and the feather duster from the broom closet. Back upstairs, he set up the shaky ladder in front of the fireplace. With the duster in his hand, he climbed to the top and then stepped off onto the marble mantel. He started to dust, whisking the feather broom back and forth over the carvings. It was a tall panel, and in order to reach the top, he had to stand on tiptoe. Whisk, whisk! Cobwebs flew in all directions. If only he could reach the top of that silly half-moon and knock off the cobweb that was trailing from one of its horns. Anthony lunged with the duster, and then something happened. There was a sharp crack, like a pistol shot. The half-moon flew off the cornice, whizzed across the room, and landed in a corner.

Anthony's face turned red. He didn't dare look at the people who were in the library. Slowly, carefully, he set the duster down on the mantel and clambered down from his perch. With his head down, he walked quickly across the floor and knelt to pick up the ornament. To his very great surprise, he saw that it had broken in two. One moon face lay staring up, and the other lay propped against a chair leg. Inside the piece that was standing up, Anthony could see something glittering. It looked like a gold coin. And between the two pieces of wood, on the floor, lay a tightly rolled piece of paper.

Chapter 3

ANTHONY knelt there, lost in wonder. The wooden moon had been like a fortune cookie, with a message inside. But what was the message? The paper lay before him. All he had to do was unroll it and read. But Anthony was a cautious sort. If the paper turned out to be anything important—a treasure map, for instance— he wanted to examine it in private. And if that really was a gold coin there . . . well, he'd better scoop it up quick before somebody else decided that it was theirs.

With trembling fingers, Anthony gathered up the two wooden fragments and the piece of paper. He glanced nervously around and then made a dash for the door. In the hall, he almost ran into Miss Eells, who had a big paper bag in her hand.

"Watch out, Anthony," she said, laughing, "or you'll

27

knock over the chocolate malt I brought you! Good grief! What do you have there?"

"It's—it's . . . I had an accident," Anthony stammered. "Can we go to your office f-for a minute?"

Miss Eells gave Anthony a wondering look. "Sure. Of course. It's snack time, anyway. Come on."

Anthony followed Miss Eells to her office. As soon as they were inside, he dumped the pieces of the ornament and the paper on her desk. Then he rushed to the door, closed it, and turned the key in the lock.

Miss Eells watched him in amazement. She glanced at the things on her desk. "Great Godfrey! Anthony, what are you up to? I shouldn't have taught you that Civil War spy code. It's gone to your head."

"I'm sorry, Miss Eells. I know it looks dumb, but I found something inside a piece of wood that I knocked off of the top of the fireplace." Anthony stopped talking when he saw the way Miss Eells was looking at him. Suddenly he was seized by the fear that he had damaged something valuable. Would Miss Eells get made at him because he had smashed the little wooden moon? "It—it was an accident," Anthony stammered, pointing to the wooden fragments on the desk. "I'm sorry, I really am, I was dusting and . . . I'm clumsy, I know I am . . ."

"Anthony, Anthony, you idiot! Did you think I would be mad at you for something like that? Good lord, you know how clumsy *I* am. Did you *really* think I would fire you for such a thing? Now, what's all this?"

"I don't know," said Anthony. "The little wooden doojiggy came apart when I knocked it down, and these things were inside it."

Miss Eells's eyes opened wide. "Were they now? Well, just sit down and make yourself homely, as my father used to say, and we'll see what's what."

28

Miss Eells sat down behind her desk. Anthony pulled up a chair. He watched with growing excitement and curiosity as she turned over the two wooden fragments. She shook the piece that had the coin in it, but the coin was wedged tight. Miss Eells reached into her desk drawer and took out a penknife. She pried at the coin, and it came clattering out onto her desk top. She picked it up and examined it.

"What is it?" Anthony asked. "It looks like it's gold."

"It *is* gold. It's a ten-dollar gold piece. Back in the old days, they used gold coins the way we use paper money today. This one's rather worn, but I would imagine it's still worth at least ten bucks at your local bank." Again, Miss Eells smiled warmly at Anthony. She was thinking, *Here is a boy whose mother has brought him up to be selfish and suspicious. She talks money money money to him, day and night. You'd think he would have stuffed this coin into his pocket the instant he saw it. Instead, he brings it to me.*

Anthony eyed the coin hungrily. "I'll take it and put it in the library fine box if you want me to," he said in a forlorn voice.

"Fine box, my eye!" said Miss Eells, laughing. "Here, Anthony, take it! Finders keepers is what I say. It's yours."

Anthony could hardly believe his ears. "R-really? Honest to God?"

Miss Eells nodded. "Honest to God. I wouldn't try to spend it at the five- and ten-cent store, but if you take it to the bank, I'm sure they'll cash it for you. If they have any questions about how you got it, tell them to call me."

"Gee, thanks," said Anthony, beaming. He stuffed the coin into his pocket.

"Now then, what *else* have we here?" said Miss Eells

as she picked up the scroll of paper and carefully unrolled it. The paper turned out to be three small sheets of onionskin paper all rolled up together. The sheets were covered with square, precise lettering.

"What is it?" asked Anthony eagerly.

Miss Eells squinted at the writing. Then she opened the middle drawer of her desk and took out a magnifying glass. "Ah, that's better. Hm . . . hmmm . . . it seems to be a message from good old Alpheus Winterborn. Want to hear what it says?"

"Sure!"

"Okay. Here goes: 'I, Alpheus Winterborn, swear that the following is a true statement. It is generally thought that I found nothing of any value during my visits to Egypt and the Holy Land. This is not true. On one trip, and under highly unusual circumstances, I discovered an object of great antiquity, an object that was at one time very sacred to one of the ancient peoples of the earth. It is an object that was thought to have perished utterly, without a trace. I returned to America with a part of that object—a part that, I daresay, is quite valuable, worth many thousands of dollars.

" 'At first I thought that I would present my discovery to a museum. But I considered further, and at length concluded that I would not. The world has rejected my efforts in the field of archeology. Well, I reject the world, and I challenge it to match wits with me. I have hidden the object I found, but I have left clues that, when read properly, will lead to its discovery. The person who finds this message is well on his way to finding the treasure I speak of. But I warn him, there's many a slip 'twixt the cup and the lip.

" 'Here, then, is the first clue. It is a poem written by myself and titled 'Mirror, Mirror.'

" 'Acorns up
      And windows over
      That will put you
      In the clover.

" 'How high is up?
      The top of the roof.
      Mind the prancing and the pawing
      Of each little hoof.

" 'Good hunting. Alpheus T. Winterborn.' "

"Well!" exclaimed Miss Eells as she laid the papers down. "Whatever on earth do you make of *that*? Eh?"

That hungry look was back in Anthony's eyes again. The note had mentioned a treasure, a treasure worth thousands of dollars. That interested him very much. "It's like a treasure map," said Anthony eagerly. "I mean, if we figure out what the poem means, we'll find the treasure he's talking about, won't we?"

Miss Eells glanced at him skeptically over the top of her glasses. "Maybe we would, and maybe we wouldn't. I hate to throw cold water on your schemes, but there's another side of Alpheus Winterborn's personality that you ought to know about. He was a great practical joker."

Anthony's heart sank. He knew what practical jokes were—dribble glasses and flowers that squirted water and stuff like that. "How—how do you mean, Miss Eells?"

"I mean, my friend, that this could all be a hoax. A wild-goose chase. That poem, for all you know, may be utterly and totally meaningless."

"Yeah, but what if there really is a treasure?" Anthony insisted.

"What if there's cheese on the moon?" said Miss

Eells sarcastically. "What if there's pie in the sky? Anthony, I don't want to seem harsh, but you don't know what that old coot was like."

Anthony suddenly felt depressed. "Are you sure it's a joke?" he said at last.

"Of course not. Good Lord, I'm not sure of anything in this life. Nobody is. I'm just telling you what I think because—well, because I don't want you to do a lot of work for nothing. I don't want you to be disappointed."

Anthony didn't seem to be listening to Miss Eells. He was staring at the little bundle of papers that lay under her hand. "Could—could I have the message?" he asked hesitantly. "I wouldn't spend a lot of time working on it, I promise. I just wanna—sort of look at it for a while." He looked hopefully at Miss Eells and waited for an answer.

Miss Eells burst out laughing. "Oh, Anthony! You're about as good at hiding your feelings as I am! If I give these papers to you, you'll go straight home and slave over them till you think you've solved the riddle. Won't you?"

Anthony's face turned red. He stared at the floor and said nothing.

"Here," she said, shoving the papers across the desk. "Take them. And if you ever figure out what that idiotic poem means, let me know. Okay?"

"Gee, thanks, Miss Eells!" said Anthony with a grin. He scooped the papers up and stuffed them into his shirt pocket. "Thanks a whole lot. I really mean it."

"Don't mention it," said Miss Eells, chuckling. She sat back in her chair and folded her arms. "My, my!" she said thoughtfully. "What a thing to find! Now we know what old Goofyblotz was doing with some of his time during that week he spent alone here in the library.

32

He was whittling a hole in that silly moon thing so he could hide his poem and the coin. Speaking of which," she said, glancing hastily at her watch, "if you want to get that gold piece changed today, you'd better hurry. It's a quarter to three, and the bank closes at three."

"Is it okay if I go? I could come right back afterward."

"Oh, there's no need for you to come back today, Anthony. Business is rather slow. Go on out and have a game of ball."

Anthony jumped up. "Gee, thanks again, Miss Eells!" he said. And then he was off on the dead run for the bank.

Chapter 4

WHEN Anthony got to the bank, he was all out
of breath. He stopped on the sidewalk outside, and as he
stood there panting, he wondered whom he ought to see
about cashing the ten-dollar gold piece. He thought
about Miss Grace, the kind and helpful teller who
always took care of his savings-account problems for him.
He hoped that she would be there today.

But when he got inside and looked around, Anthony
saw to his dismay that Miss Grace was not where she
usually was. In the past, she had always been in the
teller's cage at the end of the left-hand counter. Instead,
a tall, gloomy, balding man with a little thin moustache
was standing behind the counter with his side turned to
Anthony. He was shuffling through some papers and
scratching his upper lip. He seemed annoyed about some-

thing. Anthony was disappointed, and a little frightened. Would this man be willing to help him? He didn't look very friendly. Anthony approached the counter timidly and said, "Excuse me, sir, but could you help me?"

The man went on shuffling papers. He didn't seem to hear Anthony at all. Anthony spoke again in a louder voice. "Excuse me, sir, could you help me?"

Finally the man looked up at Anthony in an annoyed way, the way people do when they have been interrupted. "Yes? What is it?"

"Uh, excuse me, but—but . . ."

"Oh, come to the point, for heaven's sake!" the man snapped. "I haven't got all day."

Anthony's face started to get red. He felt like turning around and running out of the bank. But he took a deep breath instead and dug his hand into his pocket. He pulled out the ten-dollar gold piece and shoved it across the counter to the man. "M-Miss Eells down at the library gave me this," he said, talking very fast and staring hard at the counter. "And—and she says I can have it and that you would give me ten dollars' worth of real money for it. You can call her up and ask her if you don't believe me. It's really okay, it really is."

The man reached out and picked up the coin. And as he did this, his whole expression seemed to change. His face turned pale, and the lines around his mouth grew hard. "Where did you get this?" he asked sharply.

Anthony was startled by the way the man acted. Then he began to get frightened. Was it a counterfeit coin? He had heard somewhere that you could be put in jail for passing counterfeit money. "It's—it's real," he stammered. Then he added in a weak voice, "Anyways, I think it is. Miss Eells gave it to me. You could call her up if you want. She says it's okay."

The man said nothing. He turned the coin over in his

35

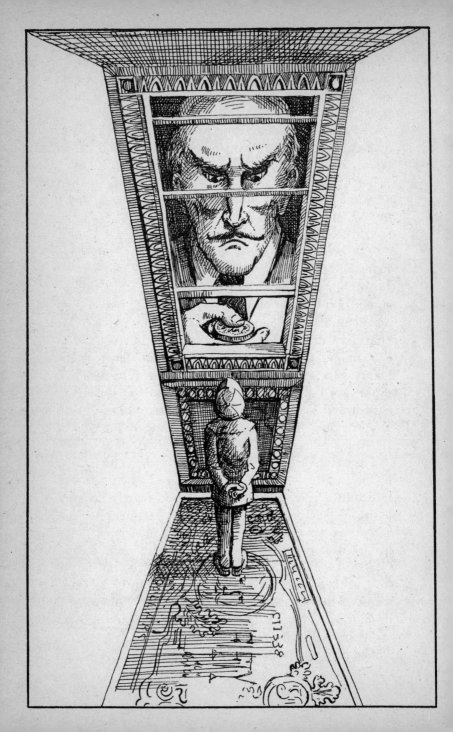

hand. He seemed to be thinking. "Excuse me, young man," he said in a cold, dignified voice. "If you don't mind, I have to take this into the back room. We have an expert here, a gentleman who knows a good deal about coins, and he may be able to tell us if—if this coin is worth more than it seems to be worth. Do you mind if I check with him?"

"Gee, no," said Anthony. "Go ahead." His face suddenly brightened at the idea that he might have a rare coin.

"I'll be back in a few minutes," said the man. He turned and left the teller's cage. Anthony heard a door open and close behind the high wooden partition. Now all sorts of doubts and fears came flooding into his mind. What if this man just pocketed the coin and pretended that Anthony hadn't given it to him? Anthony's mother was always warning him against people's tricks, telling him to count his change and watch out for anybody who offered him something for nothing. It scared Anthony to think that he might be swindled by this dignified, businesslike man. But there was nothing he could do now. The coin was gone. He just had to wait and see.

Five minutes passed. It seemed like hours to Anthony. Finally, the man came back. He smiled coldly at Anthony and shoved a crisp, new ten-dollar bill out through the bars of the teller's cage.

"Here you are, young man. I'm sorry to have kept you waiting so long, but I wanted to make absolutely sure that we were giving you a fair shake. Unfortunately, the coin is a rather ordinary one, as ten-dollar pieces go. Also, it is rather worn, and that reduces the value of such things. But ten dollars in United States money is ten dollars, after all. It's legal tender. Here you are, and as I said before, sorry to have kept you waiting."

"Thanks," Anthony mumbled as he took the bill. He didn't know whether to be happy or sad. Had the man cheated him? He couldn't tell. On the other hand, ten dollars was a lot of money as far as he was concerned. He pulled the bill back and forth between his fingers and listened to it crackle. He was already thinking about the things he would do with this money. He would hide it away in his desk and then spend it—slowly—on movies and ice cream and soda pop and candy. Sighing with satisfaction, he took out his wallet and slid the bill into it. As he was leaving the bank, it occurred to him to wonder again why the man had acted so funny when he handed him the coin. He glanced back toward the teller's cage. But the cage was empty. The man was gone.

A couple of days later, Anthony was in the West Reading Room of the library trying to raise one of the long, heavy sash windows. The window was swollen with the heat and the damp, and it just wouldn't budge. Anthony strained and struggled and grunted and groaned, but it was no use. "Oh, the heck with it!" he said out loud. He stepped back, put his hands on his hips, and glared disgustedly at the cranky window.

Miss Eells was at the other end of the room fanning herself with a copy of *Better Homes and Gardens*. There was no one in the library but Anthony and her. "Give it up, Anthony," she said with a sigh. "That blasted window won't budge until this heat wave breaks. How long has it been this hot? I swear I can't remember when I was cool."

Suddenly Anthony gave a loud exclamation. "Hey, Miss Eells! Would you come here for a minute?"

Miss Eells looked startled. "Sure," she said, and she got up and walked to the window where Anthony was standing. "Whatever is the matter?"

Anthony pointed at a man who was walking along on

the sidewalk in front of the library. "That's the man," he said. "The guy that gave me the hard time about the coin I found."

"Oh, *him*!" said Miss Eells. "Don't you know who *he* is?"

Anthony shook his head.

"That's Hugo Philpotts. He's a sort of a bigwig in this town, though he's not as big a wig as he'd like to be. You say he was standing behind the counter in the bank?"

"Yeah. He was where Miss Grace always is."

"Huh! Well, I must say that's odd. You see, he's not a clerk in that bank. He's a vice-president. Vice-presidents don't usually stand behind the counters and change money. They sit in big offices with secretaries and phones and stock tickers and everything. I wonder what he was doing behind the counter."

"Maybe he was checkin' up on somebody," Anthony said. "Maybe he thought one of the clerks was stealin' money, and so he wanted to find out for sure and catch the guy red-handed."

Miss Eells looked amused. "Maybe so," she said. "It certainly would be like him. He's a crafty, cold, sneaky old so-and-so, and he's always suspecting somebody of trying to do him out of a nickel. I hate to speak so harshly of one of the pillars of our community, but I'm afraid it's the truth. By the way, did you know he was related to our dear Alpheus?"

Anthony looked surprised. "To Mr. Winterborn?"

Miss Eells nodded. "Mm-hmmm. The same. Alpheus's sister married a man named Philpotts, and Hugo is their child. Of course 'child' is not the word—Hugo is nearly fifty now. But Alpheus Winterborn was his uncle. And in a funny way, Hugo has been living in his uncle's shadow for most of his adult life."

"I don't get what you mean."

"I mean just this: Alpheus Winterborn died in 1929, when Hugo was twenty. He left most of his money to his son, Alpheus Junior, the one who is now president of the Winterborn Silverware Company. He hardly left anything at all to his sister's family—he and his sister were on the outs at the time he died, but I forget why. At any rate, Hugo has always felt that he ought to have gotten more money from his uncle. He's felt cheated for a long time now, and I really think he believes that if old Alpheus had done what he ought to have done, he, Hugo, would be a millionaire now."

"It sure would be nice to have a million bucks," said Anthony dreamily.

"Maybe. But as my late father used to say, if a bullfrog had wings, he wouldn't bump his rear end on the ground."

Anthony laughed.

"Oh, by the way," Miss Eells said, "I hope you noticed what a nice job I did with that little wooden moon. It's all back in place again. No one would ever know it had been knocked down."

Anthony peered down toward the fireplace. "Gee, it looks great, Miss Eells. How did you get it back on?"

"Oh, it wasn't much of a problem. I just glued the two halves together. There's a little plug on the bottom of the moon, and it fits into a hole on the cornice. By the way, there wasn't a trace of glue on the plug. Alpheus must've just balanced it up there so some lucky person would knock it off accidentally."

"I don't feel so darned lucky," grumbled Anthony. "I still haven't figured out what that crummy poem is all about." He had read the poem over quite a few times since he found it, but he hadn't been able to make head or tail of it. He had even held each of the onionskin sheets over the flame of a candle for a while, just to see if there was any secret writing on them. There wasn't. "Did you tell anybody else about the stuff I found?" he asked anxiously.

Miss Eells pursed her lips disdainfully. "No, indeed. Do you think I want everybody in God's creation poking around my library looking for hidden treasures?"

"You still don't think there's a treasure at all, do you, Miss Eells?" said Anthony.

Miss Eells smiled sadly at him. "No, I don't. I'm sorry, but I really, truly don't. I know you want to find a hoard of gold coins or something like that. Who doesn't? But I won't lie to you to make you feel better. I think the poem is just Alpheus's idea of a joke, and I think you're wasting your time with it. Forget about it, Anthony. You'll feel better if you do."

Chapter **5**

ONE simmering hot day toward the middle of August, Anthony decided that he would meet his father at work and walk home with him at lunchtime. Mr. Monday worked long hours at his saloon, but he always came home between twelve and two for a leisurely lunch. When Anthony got to his dad's saloon, he went in the back way, as he always did. Kids weren't supposed to go into saloons, and Anthony always felt sneaky when he did it. At the back of the saloon were three big round tables where men were sitting, smoking cigars and pipes and talking and laughing and playing cards. Several men were standing at the long wooden bar. Overhead, two fans with broad wooden blades slowly turned, stirring the sluggish smoke. Behind the bar was his dad wearing a white apron and drawing a glass of beer. Anthony edged behind the bar and walked along to where his dad was standing.

"Hi, Dad! Gettin' ready to close up?"

"In a minute, Tony. How're things at the library?"

"Great, Dad. Just great."

Mr. Monday slid the glass of beer across the counter to a customer, then turned and smiled at Anthony. "Yeah, it feels good to work, don't it? Keep it up, kid, and maybe when you turn eighteen you can come down here and help me a bit." He added cautiously, "If you feel like it, that is."

Anthony didn't know how he felt about his dad's business. He knew that there was something not quite right about running a saloon. Kids made fun of him sometimes. They would come staggering up to him, pretending they were drunk and saying things like, "Hey, Tony, I just been to yer dad's joint!" And if it was an okay place, how come his dad called it a cigar store? Anthony had seen his dad come home at night, and he had seen how tired he looked. Anthony figured that someday, some way, he would find an easier way of making a living.

Of course, he didn't say any of this to his father. He just grinned and said, "Yeah, sure, Dad. That'd be great."

It took Mr. Monday about twenty minutes to get everybody out and close up the saloon, but before long, he and Anthony were walking along down a shady side street toward home. Anthony glanced at his dad. He thought he looked very tired and worn. The flesh of his face was sagging, and it was very pale. There were dark hollows under his eyes, and he walked with a shuffling, weary gait. Every now and then he would stop and pull out a handkerchief and mop his forehead.

"Boy, it sure is hot today!" Mr. Monday sighed.

"When I get home, I think I'll climb into the tub and take a nice cold—oh! Oh, my gosh!"

Mr. Monday stopped walking. He put his hand to his chest—to his left side, where his heart was. For a moment he just stood there, breathing heavily.

"What's wrong, Dad?" said Anthony anxiously. "How come you had to stop like that?"

Mr. Monday shook his head and started to walk on. "I dunno, Tony, I just don't know. I feel lousy these days. It must be the heat. Sometimes I feel all limp and wishy-washy, like there wasn't any strength left in my body. And then I get these pains, like just now. Right across my chest, like somebody was stickin' hot knives into me. I think I must of thrown my arm out when I was rasslin' kegs down from the truck last week."

"Maybe you oughta go see Doc Luescher, Dad. He'd find out if there was anything wrong."

Mr. Monday shrugged. "Aah, what does he know? It's just my shoulder. That's all it is. When this heat wave breaks, I'll feel better."

Mr. Monday didn't like doctors much. He was always boasting that he'd never had a sick day in his life, which was not exactly true. He got colds and the flu like everybody else, but after his illnesses were over with, he liked to think that he had cured himself. He was a kind man, but he had a streak of stubbornness in him about anything that had to do with his health.

"Dad," said Anthony after they had walked a little farther, "are you sure you don't think you oughta go see Doc Luescher?"

"Sure I'm sure," growled Mr. Monday, and he gave his son an irritated glance that meant he didn't want to talk about doctors and ailments any more.

And for the time being, that was the end of it.

———

Two days passed. The heat wave went on. The thermometer stood at eighty in the middle of the night, and during the day the sky had that yellow, brassy look that it sometimes has during heat waves. Each evening when the sun went down, it was a red ball, swimming in a sea of blue vapor.

One noontime, Anthony, his brother, and his mother were sitting around the big round table in the kitchen, waiting for Mr. Monday. They always waited till he got home before they started eating—it was one of their little family rules.

The screen door slammed. Everyone looked up. It was Mr. Monday. He stood there swaying, just inside the door, white as a sheet, with a glazed look in his eyes. His hand was clutched over his heart.

"My God, Howard, what's wrong?" Mrs. Monday exclaimed. Mr. Monday said nothing. Moving heavily and sluggishly, he stomped past the kitchen table and staggered through the living room into the front room. He was headed toward the parlor.

Anthony, Keith, and Mrs. Monday watched him with fear and astonishment in their eyes. Then they jumped up, knocking over chairs in their haste, and ran into the parlor. When they got there, they found him slumped on the couch. His face was red now, red as a beet, and he was breathing like a horse. His left arm hung limp, and with his right hand he was fumbling with his tie, trying to loosen it. His shirt was soaked with sweat, and under it his chest was going up and down rapidly.

"Oh, my God!" screamed Mrs. Monday. "Oh, my God, oh, my God, oh, my God! What is it, Howard? What happened? What happened? Oh, God, please, somebody, do something! Do something!" She threw herself down at her husband's side and started weeping hysterically.

"Jesus," said Keith in a low, awe-stricken voice. "We better call Doc Luescher. We better call him quick." He rushed to the phone and started dialing. Mrs. Monday kept on weeping, her arms around her husband's neck. Mr. Monday didn't say anything. He couldn't. He just went on panting. Anthony stood watching, horrified. He felt numb and helpless.

Twenty minutes later, Doc Luescher's big black Cadillac pulled into the driveway outside the Mondays' house. Doc Luescher was a tall, elderly man who always wore black suits that looked as if he had slept in them. His white hair was parted down the middle and lay in two even sheaves on top of his head. His face was small and square, and he had bushy white eyebrows. Anthony thought he looked like an owl.

Keith went to the door and opened it. "Hi, Doc. It's my dad," he said in a low voice, motioning toward the parlor. "I think he's had a heart attack or something. He's in there."

Doc Luescher said nothing. He just walked into the parlor, knelt down, and opened his black bag.

Mrs. Monday was sitting on a straight chair next to the couch. Her face was streaked with tears, and she had a handkerchief in her hands that she kept wadding and unwadding. Mr. Monday lay stretched out on the couch. His tie was off, and his shirt collar was open. He wasn't breathing so hard now, but his face was very pale. His eyes were closed.

Doc Luescher reached into his bag and took out a stethoscope and listened to Mr. Monday's heart. Then he took his blood pressure.

"How bad is it, Doctor?" asked Mrs. Monday anxiously.

"It's not good," said Doc Luescher as he unsnapped

the cloth from Mr. Monday's arm. "It's not good at all."

"Is it his heart, Doctor?" Keith asked.

The doctor nodded. "It sure is," he said.

Mrs. Monday began crying again. The doctor glanced sourly at her.

"Oh, don't go all to pieces, Ginny," he muttered. "People have heart attacks all the time, and this here one that Howard's had is a fairly mild one, as such things go. We've got to be careful, though. There might be another one on the way, and that's what we've got to watch out for." He folded up the stethoscope and put it away. Then he turned back to Mr. Monday. "Howard, you just lie still for now. I'm going to phone the hospital and have them send an ambulance around to take you there so we can do an electrocardiogram and some other things."

"Will I have to stay in the hospital?" Mr. Monday's voice, which was normally loud and cheerful, now sounded faint and whispery.

Doc Luescher shrugged. "Dunno. That will all depend, like they say. Just you lie there now. That's all I want you to do."

Mr. Monday did as he was told. He didn't have the strength to resist. As soon as Doc Luescher was sure that his patient was resting comfortably, he called the hospital. A few minutes later, a big white ambulance pulled up outside.

As Anthony and Keith stood watching and as Mrs. Monday sniffled loudly, two men in white uniforms got out, opened up the back doors of the ambulance, and took out a rolled-up stretcher. They came in the front door and unrolled the stretcher on the parlor floor.

"It's okay, I can walk," said Mr. Monday, and he started to get up.

47

"Relax, Howard," said Doc Luescher, gently easing him back onto the couch. "It isn't every day you get a free ride. Sit back and enjoy it."

Reluctantly, Mr. Monday lay back and let the two attendants ease him onto the stretcher. Out the door they went and down the front steps.

"Oh, what are we gonna do, what are we ever gonna do?" wailed Mrs. Monday in a choked, weepy voice.

"He's gonna be all right, Ginny," said the doctor, patting her on the back. "Don't worry now," he added, even though he knew that saying "Don't worry" to her was like saying "Don't breathe."

Mr. Monday only stayed in the hospital overnight, but when he came home, he had a fistful of prescriptions for pills he had to take, and he had strict orders from Doc Luescher: He couldn't do any work of any kind for two whole weeks. After that, the doctor promised he would check him over again and see if he could go back to work. Mrs. Monday went down to the store and taped a sign up in the plate-glass window of the front door. It said CLOSED DUE TO ILLNESS.

The awful thing had happened: Mr. Monday couldn't work.

As far as Mrs. Monday was concerned, it was the end of the world, or pretty close to it. It didn't do any good for Doc Luescher to tell her that her husband would very likely be able to go back to work someday soon. Neither did it do any good for Mr. Monday to remind his wife that they had some money in the bank that they could live on for the time being. As far as Mrs. Monday was concerned, the axe had fallen.

Not surprisingly, Anthony caught the worry bug from his mother. Fear gnawed at him, fear that his dad would never work again and that they would soon be out in the street. Miss Eells tried to reassure him, but what did she know, Anthony thought. She wasn't a doctor.

In the midst of his fear, Anthony turned to the mysterious message he had found, the message containing the poem that was supposed to be the key to a hidden treasure. He had bought a small black ring-binder and some paper at the ten-cent store and had taped each of the crackly, curly pages of the message on a separate sheet of paper. Then he put the pages in the binder. He brought the binder to work with him each day, and at odd moments he would pull it out and pore over the poem. But so far it hadn't yielded one tiny little glimmer of meaning to him. Not one.

Anthony, however, was persistent. Night after night he sat up with his desk lamp on, reading the poem over and over and over. At the library, Miss Eells would find him sitting at the circulation desk, staring fiercely at the mysterious words until the sweat ran down his face. Several times she tried to get him to quit, but he wouldn't. As far as he was concerned, the treasure of Alpheus Winterborn was his family's only hope, and he would find it or go crazy trying.

Sometimes Miss Eells was actually a bit afraid that Anthony *would* go crazy, and she began to search her brain for something that would take Anthony's mind off the treasure.

One Friday afternoon, while she was sitting in her office and reading the paper, Miss Eells noticed that there was going to be an auction out in Rolling Stone, a very small town about six or seven miles from Hoosac. Miss Eells liked auctions. She liked the crowds and poking about among pieces of furniture, and the bibble-babble of the auctioneer, and the excitement of the bidding. She decided that she would ask Anthony to go along with her.

When she found him, he was running around the East Reading Room, chasing a fly that had gotten in.

"Anthony, there's going to be an auction out in Rolling Stone tomorrow afternoon. I wondered if you'd like to go to it with me. I can get Mrs. Pratt from the branch library to take over here for the day. There'd be no problem. Afterward, we could go down the river to that new ice cream stand I told you about." Miss Eells was an expert on ice cream stands. She knew about all the good ones for miles around. "They've got a lot of good flavors, I hear," she added hopefully. "Like banana and blue moon and ginger. You don't find many stands that have ginger. Come on, what do you say? Let's give it a try, eh? Please come with me, just this once. Then you can go back to that darned poem and pore over it to your heart's content."

Anthony hesitated. He bit his lip and rattled the change in his pocket. "Okay," he said at last.

Miss Eells smiled happily and clapped her hands. "Good! That was what I hoped you'd say. Now, run on back to the main desk and see if anybody wants anything. I'll see you later."

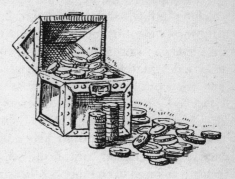

Chapter 6

THE next day, right after lunch, Miss Eells picked
Anthony up, and they drove out to Rolling Stone to the
auction. It was a beautiful day—the last day of August,
but chilly, with a hint of fall in the air. When they got
to Rolling Stone, they found that a good-sized crowd had
already gathered on the lawn of the house where the
auction was to take place. It was the house of a lady
named Bjornson, who had just died at the age of
ninety-four. Mrs. Bjornson had been a widow for the
last fifty years, and after her husband died, she had kept
her house just the way it had been around the turn of
the century. All the furniture was old-fashioned, and
there were even gas lamps on the walls, though they no
longer worked. In addition to all this, Mrs. Bjornson

had been a great buyer of antiques. She had gone to a lot of auctions in her life, and she had bought a lot of things, some of them quite valuable. Now that she was dead, her own things were being auctioned off.

Anthony and Miss Eells walked through the old, stale-smelling house, and then poked around among the furniture and other odds and ends that were scattered on the lawn, waiting to be sold. There were bureaus and commodes, marble-topped tables, oil lamps, sets of dishes and boxes of old records and a crank-up phonograph, an Atwater Kent radio, and all sorts of weird-looking doodads and whatchamacallits. Miss Eells opened and closed drawers and peered into pitchers and almost dropped a heavy, old-fashioned flatiron on her foot. Anthony got a little worried watching her because every time she turned around she would bump into somebody or something. Finally, she broke a small vase. She took the pieces up front to the auctioneer, who was just getting ready to climb up onto his stand. His name was Mr. Gegenfurtner. He was a big, red-faced man who ran a clothing store in Hoosac and did auctioneering because he liked it. He and Miss Eells were old friends. When he saw her coming toward him with the broken vase in her hands, he grinned.

"Well, hello, Myra! Did you break that Ming vase? That'll be forty-five thousand dollars, if you don't mind. Come on, hurry up. Pay."

"Oh, be quiet, Charley. How much is it worth, really?"

"I'd say about thirty-five cents. Give me a quarter, and I'll let you go. Say, who's your friend there?"

"This is Anthony Monday. He works at the library. Anthony, this is Mr. Gegenfurtner."

"Hi," said Anthony shyly.

A few moments later, Anthony and Miss Eells were

back out on the lawn, milling around with the crowd. Mr. Gegenfurtner had started auctioning things off. Anthony loved to listen to him babble: "Three, three, who'll gimmee three, threena quatta, threena quatta, quattava dollah, quattava dollah . . ." It was like a foreign language that Mr. Gegenfurtner was speaking. Anthony couldn't figure out how anybody managed to follow the bidding, but they did. People held up their hands and yelled things, and items got sold—books and pictures and tables and chairs and vases. So far, Miss Eells hadn't bid on anything. She was still inspecting the goods.

Anthony was beginning to get bored. He wandered off by himself and sat down on a glider—a kind of porch swing that looks like a sofa—that had been hauled down off the porch and left under a big elm tree. As he rocked back and forth, back and forth, he found that he was singing "Acorns *up* and *win*dows *o*-ver" in time with the squeaks. It was no use, it was just no use. He couldn't get the poem or the treasure out of his mind. . . .

Suddenly he stopped swinging. He planted both feet on the ground and stared fixedly, as if he had been hypnotized. Not far away from him was Hugo Philpotts, holding what appeared to be a small picture in a wooden frame. Hugo Philpotts, the man who had changed his ten-dollar gold piece at the bank, the man who was related to Alpheus Winterborn.

As Anthony watched, Mr. Philpotts carefully examined the picture, or whatever it was. He turned it over, and as he did so, something flashed in the sun. The thing he was looking at was a mirror. Suddenly there popped into Anthony's mind the title of Alpheus Winterborn's mysterious poem: "Mirror, Mirror." The title didn't seem to have anything to do with the poem, and once when Miss Eells was trying to help Anthony with the poem, she had guessed that the title might have something to do with an object that you were supposed to be hunting for instead.

Mr. Philpotts was really interested in this mirror. He examined the back of it and stared at one corner down at the bottom for a very long time. Finally, he set the mirror down.

When Mr. Philpotts left, Anthony slowly walked over to where the mirror lay. He knelt down and looked at it. Like Mr. Philpotts, he turned it over and examined the back, especially the lower part. Then he jumped up and ran off to get Miss Eells.

Miss Eells, however, was having her own problems— she had somehow managed to get her foot wedged into a small brown crockery jug. Two men were trying to get her out. Mr. Gegenfurtner held her down on a couch while the other man tugged at the crock. But the foot wouldn't come out.

When Anthony arrived on the scene, he was out of breath and excited. "Hey, Miss Eells, I been looking all over for you! We got to—oh, my gosh! What happened?"

"Well you may ask," groaned Miss Eells. "I was only climbing over a pile of stuff to get from one place to another, and I managed to do this to myself. Unh!" Miss Eells winced as the man tugged again. All of a sudden, the jug popped loose, and Mr. Rusk, the man who had been doing the tugging, careened off across the lawn and slammed into the back of a lady who was peering into an old chest. The lady fell forward over the chest, which snapped shut on one end of a long feather boa that she was wearing. When the lady got her wind back, she found that the trunk lid had chopped off one end of

her boa. She started to rant at Mr. Rusk, who began to rant right back at her.

Miss Eells covered her face with her hands.

"Miss Eells," said Anthony, tugging at her sleeve. "I want you to come over here and see something. It's important. It really is."

"Okay, okay! Keep your shirt on. I'll be with you in a second."

Miss Eells stopped long enough to tell Mr. Gegenfurtner that she hoped he could get through the rest of the auction without any more disasters. Then she followed Anthony across the lawn.

"Look!" said Anthony excitedly.

Miss Eells looked. What she saw was a small antique mirror. It was about two feet long and a foot wide. Mounted above the looking-glass part of the mirror was a small painting. It showed a house with a red roof and green shutters standing between two trees. The sky in the background was gray, except down near the horizon, where it was red. It looked the way the sky looks sometimes on a cloudy day just after the sun has gone down. The frame of the mirror was made of wood, and it was fairly elaborate. Across the top of the mirror ran a little ledge. It hung out over the front and sides like a canopy. The ledge had knobs on it. They were funny little knobs that looked like acorns.

"Well?" said Miss Eells. She was impatient to get back to the auction, and she was still pretty flustered.

"Look, Miss Eells, don't you see? These're the *acorns*. The ones in the poem. You said we might have to look for a mirror, and here it is!"

"I was only making a suggestion, Anthony. You can't really think that—"

"And look at this!" said Anthony. He knelt down next

to the mirror and tapped the painting. "Didja ever see windows like these? Lookit!"

Miss Eells bent over and looked closely at the painting. The house had five windows, and each one looked like this:

"My Lord!" she said. "This *is* odd. It looks like the old mansion. It used to have a red roof and green shutters. It still has these funny windows in the front with the five little panes in them."

"And how about this?" exclaimed Anthony triumphantly. He took the mirror in his hands and turned it over. There was a slab of wood on the back, held in place by bent nails. In the lower left-hand corner of the slab three letters had been scratched into the wood: ATW.

"It's him, it's Alpheus T. Winterborn," said Anthony. "Doncha see? This mirror is supposed to go with the poem! It tells how many acorns and windows there are. It all works out, like on a treasure map!" He looked hopefully at Miss Eells, who was scratching her chin and thinking.

"I don't know," she said slowly. "It may all be just a coincidence. I've seen mirrors with acorn motifs like this before. They're fairly common. As for windows, well, a house in a painting has to have windows, and I could be wrong about this being the old Winterborn house."

"Yeah, but windows that look like the five on playing cards? Didja ever see any like that? Didja? Huh?"

Anthony was beginning to feel desperate. He had

hoped that Miss Eells would feel excited, the way he did. Instead, she was skeptical. It made him mad.

Miss Eells looked at the mirror some more. She cocked her head over to the right side. Then she cocked it over to the left. "It *is* a very nice mirror," she said slowly. "In fact, it's one of the nicest of its kind that I've ever seen."

"Somebody else thinks it's nice, too," Anthony muttered. "Old Hugo Philpotts thinks it's nice. I betcha he buys it."

Miss Eells turned and stared at Anthony. "Hugo Philpotts? Is *he* at this auction?"

Anthony nodded his head firmly. "Sure. Didn't you see him? He's over there somewheres right now." Anthony pointed off toward the house. Sure enough, there was Hugo Philpotts, standing on the lawn near the front porch. He was opening and closing the doors of a large mahogany wardrobe.

Miss Eells's eyes opened wide. "Hmph! Well now, isn't that something!" She scratched her chin and pursed her lips. She seemed to be thinking. "Of course, it stands to reason," she said at last. "He collects antiques. His house is full of them. And he has a lot of money to spend on such things. On top of all that, this is a mirror that used to belong to his uncle. He must've seen the initials scratched in the corner. I imagine he'll bid on it."

"No, don't let him!" said Anthony suddenly. "I mean, don't let him get it! He might find the treasure before we do!"

Miss Eells heaved a deep sigh and shook her head. She sat down on a rocking chair that stood nearby and began rocking back and forth.

There was silence for what seemed like a fairly long time. Finally Miss Eells spoke up. "Anthony?"

"Yeah?"

"Mr. Philpotts probably doesn't want this mirror because it's connected with any treasure. He wants it because it belonged to his uncle. That's why."

"Oh, yeah? How do you know?"

"I don't know for sure. I'm just guessing, the same as you are. Anyway, if the mirror is what you say it is, he doesn't need to buy it now that he's seen it. He can just count up the acorns and the spots in the windows, can't he?"

"Yeah, he could, but what if there's something hidden *inside* the mirror that tells you where to do your counting? I mean, maybe you're supposed to count up and over on a wall someplace, and the message inside tells you where to go. He would have to have the mirror to get the message, wouldn't he?"

"Yes, assuming that there *is* a message. But you're just guessing, Anthony. Don't you see that?"

"Couldn't you just buy it and take it home and see if there are any secret messages inside?"

Miss Eells heaved a very deep sigh. She stopped rocking and got up. "Tell you what I'll do," she said. "I'll bid on it, and if the bidding doesn't run higher than thirty-five dollars, I'll take it. I've only got thirty-five dollars in my purse, and I left my checkbook at home on purpose, on account of I always spend too much money at these darned auctions. There now, will that satisfy you?"

Anthony beamed. "Sure, Miss Eells! Thanks a lot. Wait'll we get it home. We'll take it apart, and we'll *find* something. I know we will."

"Come on then," said Miss Eells, laughing. "Let's go up front and see how the bidding is going."

Mr. Gegenfurtner was in great form. He rattled off

the bids, machine-gun fashion, and one by one things disappeared from the lawn. Finally, a freckle-faced boy who worked for Mr. Gegenfurtner brought a mirror up to the auctioneer's stand. Anthony could hardly contain his excitement. He looked around to see if Mr. Philpotts was still in the crowd. He was.

"*Aaand* here," said Mr. Gegenfurtner, holding up the mirror, "we have a gen-yoo-wine antique mirror, adorned with carved wooden acorns and a lovely little painting executed on glass. Now, how much am I bid?"

And so it started. Miss Eells bid five dollars. Hugo Philpotts upped it to ten. Miss Eells said ten-fifty. Hugo said eleven. Back and forth the seesaw went. Nobody else wanted the mirror. It was just the two of them, battling it out. Miss Eells glared across at Hugo, and he glared right back at her. They had never been friends, and at that moment they were bitter enemies. Miss Eells didn't believe the mirror had anything to do with any treasure, but she was so mad at Hugo Philpotts for bidding against her that she would have bid a thousand dollars if she had had the money on her. "Pompous old clunk," she muttered under her breath. "Thinks he can have anything he wants. Well, we'll see."

"I hear twenty-five dollars from the lady down in front," bellowed Mr. Gegenfurtner, pointing with his gavel at Miss Eells. "Do I hear thirty?"

"Thirty!" called Hugo Philpotts. He looked across at Miss Eells and gave her the dirtiest look imaginable. She gave him an even dirtier one and said thirty-five. Then she leaned over and whispered to Anthony, "That's as high as I can go. I hate to let that creep have his way, but there's nothing I can do. We're sunk."

Anthony dug into his pocket. He pulled out a wadded and very wrinkled ten-dollar bill. "Here, Miss Eells," he said in a shaky voice. "I brought this along, just in case. It's the money from the gold coin. Take it, please!"

Hugo Philpotts raised his hand and said, "Forty!" in a loud, clear voice.

Miss Eells didn't know what to do. She didn't want to take Anthony's money, but it was very clear that Anthony wanted her to buy the mirror—at that moment he wanted it more than anything in the whole world. Miss Eells felt flustered and hurried. She wasn't thinking very clearly. And she was angry at Hugo Philpotts—she wanted to beat him.

"Forty dollars I'm bid for this fine, old, an-teek mirrah! For-ty dollars! Do I hear forty-five? Going once . . ."

Miss Eells hesitated a second longer. Then she quickly whispered to Anthony to go up front and tell Mr. Gegenfurtner that she wanted the bidding to stop at forty-five. It was cheating, and she knew it, but she felt that it had to be done. "Going twice," Mr. Gegenfurtner intoned. There was no other way.

Anthony was off like a shot. He raced up front and jumped onto the auctioneer's stand, grabbed Mr. Gegenfurtner's arm, and told him what Miss Eells wanted. Mr. Gegenfurtner smiled and nodded. Miss Eells was his friend, and for a friend he would do this.

Hugo Philpotts saw Anthony whispering to Mr. Gegenfurtner. He didn't know what was going on, but he was suspicious. His eyes narrowed, and his mouth grew grim.

"Forty-five dollars for the mirror!" Miss Eells called out. Her voice was loud enough for everyone to hear.

"Fifty!" roared Hugo Philpotts.

"I'm bid forty-five, do I hear fifty?" said Mr. Gegenfurtner, speaking very rapidly. "Going once, twice, three times, *sold* to the lady in the funny hat!" He stabbed his gavel in the direction of Miss Eells, who was now grinning from ear to ear.

"I said *fifty*!" Hugo Philpotts roared, cupping his hands around his mouth. "Can't you hear me, you old fool?"

Mr. Gegenfurtner paid no attention to Hugo. He tied a little yellow SOLD tag on the mirror and handed it down to Anthony. But as Anthony turned away and started carrying the mirror back to Miss Eells, Hugo Philpotts came elbowing through the crowd. He lunged forward and grabbed hold of the mirror. "Give me that, you little ragamuffin!" he snarled. "I bought it, fair and square!"

"No, you didn't! It's mine — I mean, it belongs to Miss Eells! She won it! Leggo! Help, somebody help!"

Hugo Philpotts tugged at the mirror. Anthony tugged back. At this point, several people stepped in and broke up the fight. One of them was Mr. Rusk, the man who had helped Miss Eells with the pot. He pried Hugo Philpotts's hands loose from the mirror and shoved him, rather rudely, back into the crowd. "The idea!" he said, glowering at Hugo. "Tryin' to take somethin' away from a little kid! You ought to be ashamed of yourself!"

Hugo said nothing. He just glared venomously at Mr. Rusk. Anthony bore the mirror back in triumph to Miss Eells. He was on cloud nine, and so, for the moment, was she. They had won.

Chapter 7

As they drove back to Hoosac, Anthony kept twisting around in his seat and looking at the mirror, which lay on the back seat. "Boy, Miss Eells!" he said happily. "We did it, didn't we? We really did it!"

Miss Eells said nothing. She didn't look happy. As soon as the mirror was in their hands, she began having second thoughts about the whole business. It was a fine old mirror. It was probably worth forty or fifty dollars, maybe even more. And it was very satisfying to outwit the great Mr. Philpotts, who thought everything in the world ought to go his way. But she was deeply disturbed because she felt that she was leading Anthony on toward a huge disappointment. She was still pretty convinced that there wasn't any treasure.

When they got back to Hoosac, it was a little after four o'clock. Miss Eells invited Anthony to come back to her house for tea. They could talk for a bit and look at the mirror before he went home.

Miss Eells pulled her car into the driveway. She got out and went inside, Anthony following with the mirror in his hands. Soon the little table in the kitchen was all laid out for tea. There was cheesecake with strawberries. There were blueberry muffins and toasted English muffins with butter and jam, or honey if you wanted it. There was a big brown pot of Darjeeling tea for Miss Eells, and a Coke for Anthony—who had finally admitted to Miss Eells that he didn't care for tea—in a teacup.

For a while they both just ate and drank. Finally Miss Eells put down her teacup. She pushed back her chair and stood up. "All righty," she said. "Let's settle the whole thing now, once and for all! There's a tool box down in the cellar. You know where it is. Get it and meet me in the living room."

Anthony went to get the tool box. When he got back to the living room, he found Miss Eells standing next to the mirror, which was propped up on the sofa.

"Hammer," she said solemnly, holding out her hand.

Anthony gave her the hammer. She turned the mirror over and with the claw part of the hammer began prying loose the nails that held the back of the mirror to the frame. Finally, the last nail was out, and Miss Eells carefully lifted the slab of wood. Then she gasped. There, glued to the inside of the slab, was an old, yellowed envelope.

"Oh, my Lord!" exclaimed Miss Eells.

"Wow!" said Anthony.

With trembling fingers, Miss Eells pried the envelope away from the wood. The glue was old, so it didn't take too much work. She opened the envelope with her

64

thumb, which was her usual method of opening letters. Inside was a note. It was written in the square, precise lettering that Anthony was very familiar with by now. It said:

> If you have landed on the moon, the following may be of interest: Is five times five twenty-five? "X" marks the spot. Always drive on the right side. In my father's house are many mansions.
>
> Regards,
> Alpheus T. Winterborn

Anthony was jubilant. He ran around the room waving the paper and yelling "Whee!" at the top of his voice. Miss Eells just sat on the sofa with a dazed look on her face. She hardly knew what to think.

"I told you, Miss Eells!" Anthony crowed. "Look at it! Wow! Yay! Whoopee!"

Miss Eells smiled faintly. If there was a treasure, she wanted Anthony to find it. And she had to admit that this discovery was encouraging. When Anthony had stopped yelling and stomping around, she said quietly, "Could I see the note?"

Anthony handed the paper to Miss Eells. She read it over several times, then put it down on the sofa.

"Anthony?" she said at last.

"Yeah, Miss Eells?"

"If you put this note together with the one you found in the little moon, and add the features on the outside of the mirror—the acorns and the windows, I mean— you get this, at least the way I read it: Winterborn is saying that in his house—the house his father built—in the upper right room, five, or maybe twenty-five paces along the right wall, there is an "X" on the wall, or maybe on the floor. And inside the wall there, or under the floor, there is something—"

"Yeah, a treasure," said Anthony excitedly. His eyes shone as he thought of it.

"Maybe," said Miss Eells, pursing her lips. "Maybe. But there are still some things that worry me. There's more to that poem, isn't there? How does it go?"

Anthony had read the poem over so many times that he knew it by heart. "You mean the end part?

> " 'How high is up?
>   The top of the roof.
>   Mind the prancing and the pawing
>   of each little hoof.' "

"Well, how does what you just recited fit in with the rest? It doesn't, does it?"

"Gee, I guess not," said Anthony. He thought a minute. "Maybe that part was just there to throw us off. You said Mr. Winterborn liked to play jokes."

Miss Eells looked worried. She bit her nails. "Yes, he did. That's why I'm still not sure we're on the right track. There's something we're not getting. In that other note you found, he warns us that there's many a slip 'twixt the cup and the lip. I wonder . . ."

Anthony was beginning to feel irritated. Here they had just made this big discovery, and what was Miss Eells doing? Throwing on cold water, like always.

"Aw, come on, Miss Eells! Don't be such a party-pooper! We're gonna be rich!" That old dreamy, hungry look came back into Anthony's eyes. "Gosh, I wonder what it is?" he mused. "Maybe it's a gold crown, or a diamond ring that some old king used to wear. Wahoo! We're gonna be rolling in dough!" He started to dance around the room again with the piece of paper in his hand, but he stopped when he saw how gloomy Miss Eells looked. "What's wrong now?" he asked.

"Come over here and sit down, Anthony." She patted the seat of the couch beside her.

Anthony sat down.

"Now, then. There are several things in this whole deal that you don't seem to be aware of. In the first place, if there really is a treasure, and if it's hidden in Alpheus Winterborn's old house, then you may have a bit of a problem getting it out."

"How come?"

"Well, it so happens that there are people living in that house. There's a dentist and his wife and eight kids. Now, what are you going to do, Anthony? Go up to the front door and knock and say, 'Excuse me, folks, but would you mind if I came in and tapped on your walls for a bit? I'm looking for a hidden treasure'? Is that what you'd do?"

"I guess not," Anthony said sheepishly.

"You're darned right you wouldn't. They'd either think you were crazy, or start hunting themselves. Either way, you wouldn't get in."

"We could break in at night, like burglars," Anthony suggested.

"Oh, sure. It works great in the movies, but in real life . . . well, aside from it's being *illegal*, can you imagine creeping around a house that has ten people sleeping in it? Sneaking and trying not to wake them up? And with *me* as an assistant? Can you imagine what a great burglar's assistant I would make?" Miss Eells had to laugh. She couldn't help it. The idea of her as a burglar seemed very funny.

Anthony wasn't amused. He was getting angrier and angrier as Miss Eells shot down all his great ideas one by one. "Well, maybe they'll go on vacation sometime," he said at last, in a faint but stubborn voice. His lower lip started to quiver. He was struggling now to keep from crying.

Miss Eells looked up at him, and *her* eyes filled with tears. She leaped up from the couch and started toward him. "Oh Anthony, I'm sorry, I—"

"Heck with you!" Anthony shouted. He turned away and rushed out of the house, slamming the door behind him.

Chapter 8

LABOR DAY came, and school began again. Anthony was in the eighth grade now, and he had a new teacher, Miss Johansen. She was okay as far as Anthony was concerned, and it looked as if they would get along fine. But after the first month of school had passed, she told Anthony that she felt he just wasn't applying himself. Anthony knew that this was true. He had never been a top student, but now he was going completely down the tubes. During work periods, he doodled acorns and windows on his paper, or else he would make imaginary floor plans of the Winterborn mansion and dream up break-ins and burglaries. He saw less and less of his friends.

At the Monday home, things had gone from bad to

69

worse. After a month and a half of idleness, Mr. Monday decided that he was going back to work. Doc Luescher argued with him, telling him that he wasn't ready to go back yet. But Mr. Monday stubbornly insisted that he was fit and raring to go. The very first day he opened the saloon, he had another heart attack. It was a minor one, but it was enough to send him to the hospital and then back home to bed. Gloom deepened at the Monday house. Now it looked as if Anthony's dad would never get back on the job.

So Anthony continued to worry, and his dreams of treasure continued to take up most of his time. He started haunting the old Winterborn place.

The Winterborn mansion was on Front Street. It faced a large square park known as Monument Square. The house had eight sides. Several octagonal houses were built in America in the 1890s, and this was one of them. It had a domed roof and a silly little cupola on top that looked like a saltshaker. A lot of wooden doodads that looked like giant acorns hung from the eaves. The house was solidly built of brick, and it had a large backyard with swings and slides and a sandbox. Once there had been an iron fence around the whole yard, but it had long since rusted to pieces. Now only bushes guarded the house from the kids who cut back and forth across the yard on their way to and from school.

You might have thought that Mr. Winterborn's son, Alpheus Junior, would be living in the house, but he had never liked it, and as soon as his father was dead and buried, he sold it and auctioned off most of the furniture. That was how Mrs. Bjornson came to get the mirror with the acorns on it. The house had passed through a series of owners, but now it was owned by a dentist named Harold Tweedy, a friendly-looking man with glasses and curly red hair. Sometimes Anthony saw Dr. Tweedy going in or out of the house with one or two of his kids. The Tweedys had a big German shepherd dog. It lived in a doghouse that stood up against the side of the house next to the cellar door. The dog's name, Prince, was painted over the door of the doghouse. Prince was friendly to the Tweedy kids, but he barked ferociously at anyone else who passed by the house.

Night after night, as he was returning home from his job at the library, Anthony would go out of his way so he could walk past the old house. It was October now, and the nights were chilly. Anthony, with his leather jacket zipped up and his red leather cap pulled down low over his face, would amble past, looking the place over like a burglar casing the joint before a break-in. Sometimes he would stand across the street for a while, under the trees of the park, before he moved in for a closer look. The house stood fairly close to the street, so when the lights were on at night, Anthony could see in. Sometimes he would see a girl with blond hair playing the piano in the parlor. The other room at the front of the house was the dining room. The Tweedys never pulled their draperies shut, so it was easy to see into the dining room at night. Sometimes the Tweedys had dinner by candlelight. Anthony would see the candles glowing and people laughing and talking and having a good time. It made him feel jealous. Dr. Tweedy was already rich, and what was worse, he was sitting on top of a fortune that he didn't even know about. What if he found it some day by accident? Anthony didn't like to think about that.

At night, sometimes, Anthony had dreams in which he sneaked in the old house through a cellar window and crept upstairs. Moonlight lay on the walls, and everyone was asleep. In the spare room upstairs on the right, Anthony walked twenty-five steps from the front window and there on the wallpaper was an "X." But then it changed into five acorns and as Anthony watched, the five acorns changed into twenty-five "X" marks. The "X" marks turned into little windows shaped like the five-spots in a deck of playing cards. With his handy wallpaper cutter, Anthony the burglar noiselessly drew a circle. The paper fluttered away to the floor. Now he was hacking at the plaster with a noiseless electric chisel —his own invention. Bits of plaster flew in all directions. And then it was like hitting the jackpot on a slot machine. Coins—ten-dollar gold pieces, a whole stream of them—silently pouring out of the hole in the wall, glittering, bouncing, spinning into a pillowcase he had brought with him. Then he tiptoed down to the cellar, climbed out the window, and went home. But when he got back and dumped the sack out on the kitchen table in front of his mother, all that came out was a whole lot of acorns. That was when Anthony woke up.

One day when he was walking past the mansion on his way to work, he stopped because there was a truck in his way, a big truck that was backed in across the sidewalk. The truck was yellow, and on its side was a picture of an old-fashioned sailing ship. The big green letters said "Mayflower Van Lines." A long ramp had been thrown down. It ran from the back of the truck to the front door of the house, and two burly men in gray uniforms were grunting and groaning as they shoved a big upright piano along it. *The Tweedys were moving!*

Anthony could hardly believe it. Wild, uncontrollable joy leaped up inside him. Now the treasure was his, or would be, as soon as everyone had cleared out. He and Miss Eells would be able to sneak in and poke around till they found what they were looking for. Plans started racing through his mind. They would jimmy a door open or break a window. It wouldn't take long to find the right room. The house would be empty. Nobody would know.

Anthony stood watching the moving men at their work for a few minutes, delighted yet anxious. Were the Tweedys really going? He watched some more, as if he were trying to prove to himself that all this was really happening.

Finally he snapped out of his trance. If he didn't hurry, he would be late. He started walking fast, and then he started to run. By the time he got to the library, he was out of breath. He had to see Miss Eells right away. This was important news. He pushed open the front door and raced up the little flight of inside steps that led to the main floor of the library. He pushed open the swinging glass doors, and then he stopped. Directly before him, sitting at the main desk, was Miss Eells. She looked pale and drawn, and there was a white bandage around her head.

"Oh, my gosh, Miss Eells! What happened?" shouted Anthony.

Miss Eells groaned and held out a copy of the *Hoosac Daily Sentinel*. "Here," she said, "you can read about it yourself. I got broke in on. I mean, there was a burglar in my house last night."

Anthony was thunderstruck. He took the paper from Miss Eells's hand and opened it up. On the front page was a column with the headline "Break-in on Pine Street." Anthony read what was written underneath.

Sometime last evening, a break-in took place at the home of Miss Myra Eells, at 611 Pine Street, Hoosac. Miss Eells, according to the statement she submitted to the Hoosac Police Department this morning, was returning to her home after attending a movie when she saw that her front door was ajar. Thinking perhaps that the wind had blown it open, she went in, and then, in her own words, she "got an almighty crack on the skull." She was hit, Miss Eells opines, from behind. When she awoke a few minutes later, Miss Eells found the furnishings of her living room in great disarray. However, the only thing that seemed to be missing was an antique mirror that she had recently bought at an auction. When asked why she thought anyone would steal the mirror, Miss Eells said, "I guess they thought it was valuable." She declined to speculate why nothing else in the house, including her jewel box and a cookie jar containing $32.12 in small change, had been touched. Officer Earl Swett, who answered Miss Eells's call for help, ventured the opinion that the burglary was the work of an amateur. Miss Eells, who is well known as the head librarian at the Hoosac Public Library, was taken to Ferncrest Memorial Hospital. Her head, after being examined, showed nothing serious, and she was later released.

Anthony looked up. "My gosh! I bet it was that old—"

Miss Eells put her finger to her lips. "Sshh! Not out here in the open where people can hear you! Come on. Let's go back to my office."

Anthony followed Miss Eells to her office. When they got there, she closed the door and went into the bathroom. Anthony heard a door slam softly, and when Miss Eells came out, she had two bottles of Coke with her. "I've decided to go over to your side," she explained as she opened the bottles. "I've had so much trouble making tea that I decided to try something a little easier. I had an icebox installed in here, and I've stocked it with soft drinks."

Miss Eells shoved one of the bottles over to Anthony, but he didn't take it. He just sat there on the edge of his chair, looking worried. "Miss Eells," he said, "I betcha a hundred dollars it was old Philpotts that broke into your house."

Miss Eells nodded sadly. "It kind of looks like it, doesn't it?" She took a sip of Coke.

Anthony stared at her in amazement. Why was she taking this all so calmly? "How come you don't tell the cops, then? They'd go over to his place and find the mirror and throw him in the clink, wouldn't they?"

"They might," said Miss Eells dryly. "*If* they thought he were guilty. That is, if they found evidence he was guilty. But what if they didn't find the mirror, or any other evidence that would prove he was the culprit? There are laws against making false accusations, you know. You can get thrown in jail yourself if you accuse someone falsely. Besides, he's one of the leading members of our community. How would it look if I accused him of being a burglar? It would be like accusing the mayor of being a chicken thief."

"But he did it," Anthony said angrily. "I know he did."

"Oh, I'm sure you're right," said Miss Eells. "But my feeling at the present time is, let him have the stupid mirror. He didn't get the message that was inside it—that's locked up in my desk, and he never went near my desk. Boy, will he be livid when he sees that glue spot on the inside of the mirror backing and figures out that he's missed out on something. He'll be fit to be tied!"

"Do you think he knows?" asked Anthony anxiously. "About the treasure, I mean."

"It's beginning to look that way," mused Miss Eells.

She took another sip of Coke. "Hmm, I wonder how he found out? Oh, well. No matter. Like I say, let him have the mirror. It won't do him any more good than it's done us. He may have guessed by now that the treasure is in his uncle's house—if, of course, it really *is* a treasure, and not a box of Cracker Jack." Miss Eells suddenly laughed. "Hmph! Wouldn't it be funny if Hugo got so worked up over that treasure that he bought his uncle's place so he could poke around inside it? Wouldn't that be something!" She threw back her head and laughed but then she winced. The laughter had made her head hurt.

"What if there *is* a treasure, and old Philpotts gets his hands on it?" Anthony asked nervously.

"Then he'd be even richer than he is now, and not a bit happier, I'll bet. Isn't it odd that a man who already has a fair-sized pile of money should want an even bigger pile? Yet all over the world people who have enough money to live comfortably are grasping for more. Wearing themselves out, fretting, worrying, ruining their health, and for what?"

Anthony wasn't listening to Miss Eells. "I—I came over here to tell you that the Tweedys are moving out," he said, "and—"

"Yes, I know," said Miss Eells placidly. "I've known it for some time. It seems that a dentist up in Minneapolis died suddenly, and Dr. Tweedy has been invited to move up there and take over his practice. It's a nice neighborhood, and he'd be a fool to pass up the chance."

Anthony looked hurt. "If you knew they were moving, how come you didn't tell me, huh?"

Miss Eells looked straight at Anthony over the top of her glasses. "Because, my friend, I knew that once you heard the Tweedys were moving, you'd be in here pestering me to help you burglarize the place. Am I right?"

Anthony blushed and stared at the floor. "Yeah, I guess so," he said in a low voice.

Miss Eells took another sip of Coke and pushed her chair back. "I'm sorry, Anthony," she said gently. "I know you want to get at that treasure. But even with the Tweedys gone, how will you be able to do it? There's Mrs. Speece, old Eagle Eye, the lady who lives next door. She's still there. And there are the people who walk by the house all the time. *And* the house will be locked up tighter than a drum. What do you know about jimmying a window? Can you use a glass cutter? No way at all."

Anthony sat sullenly listening as Miss Eells spoke. Finally he finished his Coke and went back out front to mind the circulation desk. Half an hour later Miss Eells came out and told him that she had a splitting headache —the goose egg on her head was throbbing like anything—and that she had decided to go home and lie down. She had called Miss Pratt, the woman from the branch library, who had promised to come right over. Miss Pratt showed up fifteen minutes later, and Miss Eells went home. Anthony told Miss Pratt that he was going down to the storage room to straighten up the piles of magazines. This was a fib. He was going downstairs so he could climb upstairs to the secret room—in the tower.

Chapter 9

T HE FOUR-STORY tower that stood at the northwest corner of the library had fascinated Anthony ever since he had started working there. It was mysterious. In fact, it was like one of Alpheus Winterborn's riddles. Although it was built onto the corner of the building, you couldn't get into it from any of the rooms, upstairs or down, that were in the part of the library that touched the tower. There were no doors on the outside of the tower, either. At first, Anthony thought that the whole silly thing was sealed off from the outside world, like a tomb. But when he asked Miss Eells if there was any way to get into the tower, she merely smiled mysteriously and said, "Keep looking. You'll find a way."

Finally, about two weeks after he had started his job,

he found a way to get in. In the furnace room, behind the furnace, he had found a door with a cardboard sign tacked on it. The sign said BROOM CLOSET. But he thought this was a funny place for a broom closet, so on a hunch he took down the sign, and underneath he saw peeling gilt letters that simply said STAIRS. Nearby, on a rusty nail, hung a key. It fit the lock on the door. Behind the door was a flight of stone steps that corkscrewed up four stories to a small, round room at the top. Ever since that day, the tower room had become one of Anthony's favorite places. He went there a lot when business in the library was slow or when he just wanted to sit and think.

Right now, Anthony definitely wanted someplace where he could just sit and think. A lot of things had happened to him in a very short space of time, and his head was in a whirl. The Tweedys were moving. Miss Eells's house had been broken into, and the mirror had been stolen. Anthony climbed the steps to the top of the tower like somebody lost in a dream. When he got to the top, he opened a low, pointed door and went into the tower room. He sat down cross-legged on the floor and looked around.

There was no furniture in the room. Dust and the tiny bodies of dead insects covered the floor. Over in one corner, near a window, lay a pile of old magazines.

The tower room, when you came to think of it, was pretty useless. There wasn't even an electric light in it, or an outlet where you could plug one in. In the middle of the ceiling was a trap door. Anthony had never opened it, but he figured it led up to the roof of the tower. When the wind blew hard, he could hear the weather vane rattling overhead. The room had nine oval windows. Today, the gray light of an overcast October day filtered in through the grimy panes. Anthony sat there, motionless, looking out. Away on the western horizon ran a long line of bluffs. Below him he could see the tops of bare trees, the walks and benches of Levee Park, and the leaden gray waters of the river flowing past. Even on a dull day like this, Anthony enjoyed being up here. He felt like some ancient king surveying his kingdom.

He was deep in thought as he sat there. What on earth was he going to do? What if Hugo Philpotts *did* buy the house? Anthony didn't know how much houses cost, but he had once heard his dad say that he had paid twelve thousand dollars for the house they were living in. And that was a long time ago. Alpheus Winterborn's message said that the treasure he had hidden was worth many thousands of dollars. "Many" was more than twelve—Anthony was sure of that. So even if Hugo Philpotts had to spend twelve thousand dollars to get a treasure that was worth a hundred thousand, or a million, it would be a good deal for him. And once he bought the house, he wouldn't have to worry about old Eagle Eye. It would be his house, and if he wanted to poke holes in the walls, that would be his business. Anthony had to get in there before Mr. Philpotts did. But how in heck was he going to do that?

He continued to sit and think, but no ideas came to him. The wind blew, and the weather vane thrummed overhead. After a while, Anthony heaved a deep sigh and got up. He had better go downstairs and see if Mrs. Pratt wanted him to do anything. As he was leaving the room, he glanced at one of the magazines on the dusty stack. Some words on the cover caught his eye: "Burglar-proof Your Home This Summer. See page 106."

Anthony flipped to page 106 and started reading. The article gave thirteen rules for homeowners, including such things as not letting milk bottles and newspapers pile up on your porch, notifying the police when you went on vacation, and leaving lights on in the house. Rule Ten interested Anthony very much.

Rule Ten: On doors with old-fashioned locks, there is usually a plate (on the doorpost) with two holes. It looks like this:

The lower hole, the oblong one, is meant to receive the door latch, which moves when the knob is turned. The upper hole, square in shape, is meant to receive the bolt, which turns when the key is turned in the keyhole. It is the upper hole that we are concerned with. A favorite trick of burglars is to insert a chip of wood in this hole so that the bolt, when thrown home by the turning of the key, will not enter the hole. The door, thus tampered with, is not locked and may be opened at the convenience of our friend the burglar. It would be well to check the outside doors of your home nightly to make sure they have not been tampered with. Cellar doors in particular are vulnerable. Note any suspicious persons prowling about in your yard, as they may be burglars looking for a chance to "fix" your door in the manner described above.

Anthony sat on the heap of magazines, reading by the fading light. His heart started beating faster. *This was the way!* Could he . . . Of course he could. He would have to, to save his family and to keep old Hugo Philpotts from grabbing the loot. He would bide his time, watch carefully, and then . . .

For the next several days, Anthony carried around a small chip of wood in his pocket. He had whittled it to fit the bolt-hole in the outside cellar door of his own house. He had tried out the trick, and he had been delighted to discover that it really worked. Now he kept closer watch than ever over the old Winterborn place. The moving truck was gone now. The house looked deserted. The shades were all pulled down. The swing set was gone from the backyard. So was the sandbox, but the doghouse was still there. It looked forlorn and empty. A FOR SALE sign was tacked up on the front of the house. One day when Anthony walked by to see how things were going, he saw a big red panel truck parked outside. The lettering on the side of the truck said LOOMIS AND SON, PAINTERS AND INTERIOR DECORATORS. The front door of the house was open, and Anthony could see men inside. They were wearing gray paint-stained coveralls and paint caps. They were spreading out a drop cloth on the hall floor. Another man was taking a ladder and some cans of paint out of the back of the truck.

Anthony was panic-stricken. What if these guys started taking the wallpaper off the walls and then discovered . . . no, no. That simply couldn't happen. *Doncha see, you dumb clunk*, he said to himself excitedly, *this is your big chance! They're gonna be opening up doors all over the house. Maybe they'll open up the cellar door. Then you can do what you want to do.*

Trying hard to act nonchalant, Anthony sauntered around to the side of the house. The cellar door was directly opposite Mrs. Speece's house. Mrs. Speece, otherwise known as old Eagle Eye. It was a solid-looking black door that stood at the bottom end of a stone ramp. The ramp and its stone-lined sides formed a kind of ditch, and the ditch was full of dead leaves. Anthony checked the door. Nope. It was still shut tight. Darn! But then, as he stood there watching, the doorknob turned. The door rattled and then moved inward. A few leaves fluttered in onto the cellar floor.

Anthony felt extremely nervous. His heart was going like a trip hammer. The door was ajar, but whoever had opened it hadn't come out. Maybe somebody was painting the basement and wanted the door open for air. Slowly, Anthony began to shuffle forward. His hand was in his pocket now. It closed around the little chip of wood. He edged down the little sloping ramp that led to the door. Dry leaves crackled under his feet. Now he was at the door. He peered inside. Nobody around. Good. Quick as a flash, he pulled out the chip of wood, stuck it into the bolt-hole, and stepped back. And at that moment, somebody behind him said, "Hey, kid! What the hell you think you're doin', huh?"

Anthony froze. He jammed both hands into his pockets as if to prove that he hadn't been doing anything with them. Then he turned around. Out by the street, next to the truck, was a man in coveralls. He was smoking a cigar. It was Mr. Loomis. Anthony had seen him in his father's saloon a number of times. His dad and Mr. Loomis were old pals—sort of. At least Anthony hoped so.

"I—I wasn't doin' nothin', Mr. Loomis! Honest I wasn't!"

The man's face softened when he saw that it was Anthony. "Oh, it's you, Tony. Look, sorry to holler at you, but there's been a bunch of kids pokin' around here today makin' life difficult for me. Did you want something?"

"Uh, no, I didn't, Mr. Loomis," Anthony mumbled. He shuffled awkwardly up the ramp and started walking across the lawn toward Mr. Loomis. "I just, uh, I mean, I sorta wanted to see what the inside of this old house looked like."

"Casin' the joint, hey?" said Mr. Loomis. He laughed and patted Anthony on the back. Anthony stiffened. "Say, tell me, are you the burglar that busted into old Missus Eells's place? Come on, fess up! I got the goods on ya!"

Anthony's face got very red. He said nothing.

Mr. Loomis puffed at his cigar and laughed hoarsely. "Just kiddin', Tony, just kiddin'! Look, sometime when I don't have a lot to do, I'll show you around this dump. It's a weird old place. All the rooms are funny-looking inside on account of the house has eight sides. But right now I'm busy as heck. See ya later." He threw his cigar into the gutter, stepped on it, and turned away toward the house.

"Okay, Mr. Loomis. See you later." Anthony turned and started walking away fast. As he walked, he wondered if Mr. Loomis had seen him stick the chip of wood into the door. From the way Mr. Loomis had talked, Anthony figured that he probably hadn't. Now he began to feel very smug and proud of himself. He had pulled a real burglar's trick, and he had gotten away with it. Of course, the thought of actually breaking into somebody's house frightened him. He had always been a very law-abiding boy. But here he was, planning to break into somebody's house! That was a crime, a burglary. Did that mean he was turning into a criminal? No, Anthony told himself firmly. It was only going to be this once.

Days passed. October turned into November. Now that he had set things up for the big break-in, Anthony was developing cold feet. It was one thing to stick a piece of wood in a door, and something else to be a real-life burglar. Night after night, as he walked home from the library, Anthony thought, *I could do it now. I really could.* But then he would say to himself, *No, it's not late enough. Old Eagle Eye will be awake. She'll see. Besides, I need to have tools. I need a mallet and a chisel and some other stuff.* (He could have gotten these tools from his dad's tool chest in the garage, but he hadn't yet gotten around to taking them.) He would make other excuses to himself, excuses of all kinds. Then he would bite his lip and call himself a coward because he was afraid of old Eagle Eye. He began to think that maybe he would never get up the courage to do what he wanted to do.

Late one cold November night, Anthony lay awake in his bed. Downstairs, his folks were arguing—the old familiar scene. For a while, the arguments had stopped because Mr. Monday had been too sick to stay up late at night. But now his health was returning, and that was one of the things that tonight's argument was about— Mr. Monday's health. Mr. Monday was planning to open up the store again whether Doc Luescher gave him the go-ahead or not.

Anthony lay there, wide-eyed, listening to the battle. He began to torture himself with accusations. As far as he was concerned, this fighting and bickering was his fault. If he had only had the guts to go down and get that treasure out, they would be rich, and everything would be fine. After all, the burglary was all set up. All he had to do was push a door open and walk in. But he just couldn't force himself. He was scared of getting caught.

The argument was over. Anthony could hear chairs scraping around. His folks were coming up to bed. The shelf clock in the front hall struck eleven, then twelve, then one. But Anthony still lay there motionless, wide awake under the covers. Then, with a sudden motion, he flung back the sheet and the blankets. He sat up, swung around, and put his feet on the floor. He padded noiselessly over to the closet, put his shirt and pants on over his pajamas, and laced up his tennis shoes.

How he managed to get down to Front Street, Anthony never remembered. It was as if the whole thing were happening in a dream, as if some force outside himself were moving him around from place to place. All he knew was that sometime after he got dressed and slipped out of the house, he was down on Front Street and crouching behind a bush in the side yard of the old Winterborn place, shivering with the cold. And he was mad at himself because he hadn't brought any tools with him. His heart was beating fast, and his body felt prickly all over. His blood was pounding in his ears. He felt very strange, but he was *there*, he was at the house. That was all that mattered. As for the tools, men had been working in the house, and they had probably left some lying around. If not, he would dig the treasure out of that wall with his nails if he had to.

Anthony crouched there, staring at the cellar door. He could see it clearly by the light of the street lamp. Behind him was the house of old Eagle Eye. It was completely dark. Anthony felt his body grow tense. He clenched his fists. He stood up and started walking across the frozen grass toward the house. He walked with swift, resolute strides. He was almost there . . .

And then something happened.

Anthony heard a loud barking sound. A growling dog was rushing at him. It had leaped out of the doghouse that stood near the back porch—the doghouse that was

supposed to be empty now! Anthony screamed, "No, no! Help!" Then he turned and ran, hell for leather, across the backyard of the Winterborn house and across Mrs. Speece's backyard. Suddenly, as he was about to cross the sidewalk that ran from Mrs. Speece's back door to her garage, his feet flew out from under him. He felt as if someone had grabbed him by the ankles and flipped his legs upward.

He fell onto the sidewalk, which was sunk between two banks of grassy earth. He fell awkwardly, with his right arm pinned across his belly and his left hand thrust out to break his fall. He landed with a sickening thud and lay there in a daze. His body stung all over. The heel of his left hand was scraped, and it burned like fire. Warm blood was oozing out of it. In the distance, the dog was still barking. Anthony shook his head and groaned. He felt sick. Then he tried to raise himself on his right arm, but the arm wouldn't move.

The dog went right on barking, but it didn't follow him. It was a stray that had crept into Prince's old doghouse to get out of the cold and was trying to defend its right to stay. Anthony didn't know that, of course. He was bruised and shaken, and scared and cold and shivering. Using his left hand, he dragged himself to his knees. He shook his head groggily and looked around. Up above him, at the top of the low bank he had just fallen down, was a wire. It glimmered faintly in the light from the distant street lamp. A trip wire. Mrs. Speece had rigged it up because she had gotten tired of having kids cut across her backyard.

Anthony staggered to his feet. He put his left hand under his right forearm to hold it up. He had the very strange and terrifying feeling that if he took his hand away, his right arm would drop off. He looked at it as if he had never seen it before. It still seemed to be attached. But it was useless. It wouldn't move, and a dull pain was spreading through it. He shook his head groggily. The dog barked some more, louder now, and then a light came on in an upstairs window of Mrs. Speece's house. Anthony was so shaken and confused that all thoughts of burglary and treasure had been driven right out of his mind. All he wanted to do was get away from Mrs. Speece's house before she discovered him.

He stumbled up the second bank, checked to make sure there wasn't a second trip wire—there wasn't—and walked quickly out to the sidewalk, across the little side street, and then across Front Street to the park. He started trotting along one of the long diagonal walks that crossed the park. Confused and jumbled thoughts were running through his head: *What am I doing out here anyway? I must've been out of my mind. . . . This is all a weird dream. . . . I'll wake up any minute now. . . . Wasn't it funny about that dog? What the heck was he doing there? There wasn't supposed to be any dog in that doghouse. Maybe they left him behind when they moved . . .*

A sharp pain shot through his arm and shoulder. The pain cleared his head. It shook him out of the dreamy, numb state he had been falling into. He had better go get help. Now, as he began to get his bearings, he realized that he was closer to Miss Eells's house than he was to home. He started walking faster. He walked from one pool of lamplight to another, and dead leaves scuttled past him as he went.

He crossed the park and started up Hannah Street. He was headed toward Miss Eells's house now. His arm burned, and he felt feverish. Now the dreamy state was coming back. All sorts of weird fantasies flitted through his mind. He wondered, *Is gangrene setting in? Will they have to cut my arm off?* He had watched westerns on TV where men had their legs cut off. They always gave them whiskey to drink and made them bite hard on pieces of leather. A vague terror began to grow in his mind. Would his arm be all right?

He walked on through the silent streets, holding his arm carefully in front of him like a parcel. When he got to Miss Eells's house, he went up on the porch and rang the bell. He rang it three, four, five, ten times, pushing the button hard and holding it in for a long time. *Oh, please answer, Miss Eells*, he sobbed to himself. *Please be there, please be there. Oh, somebody do something, please do something . . .*

The porch light went on. He heard Miss Eells fumbling with the lock. Then the door opened, and Miss Eells was standing there in her bathrobe and slippers. Her glasses were stuck crookedly onto her nose. She looked crabby at first, as people often do when they have just been awakened. But then her mouth dropped open.

"Good Lord, Anthony! What are *you* doing here at this hour?"

"I—I—my arm," stammered Anthony. His eyes were stinging. "I think I've broken my arm. . . ."

Chapter **10**

Miss Eells made Anthony sit down on the couch in the living room. Then she went out to the hall and picked up the phone. She dialed the Mondays' number. The phone rang a long time, but finally somebody answered. It was Mrs. Monday. She sounded sleepy and annoyed.

"Hello, Mrs. Monday. This is Myra Eells. I really don't quite know how to tell you this, but about two minutes ago Anthony showed up at my door. No, I don't know any more than you do what he was doing out at this hour. Just calm down and listen to me. I think he's broken his arm. Yes, that's right, his arm. I'm going to drive him down to the—well, how do I know how he broke it? Please be calm and listen. I'm going to drive him down to the hospital. I'll see you down there.

Okay?" Without waiting to hear what else Mrs. Monday had to say, Miss Eells hung up.

When Miss Eells got back to the living room, Anthony was still sitting there on the couch, holding his arm and looking frightened. She sat down on the couch next to him and laid her hand gently on his knee. "Anthony?"

"Yeah, Miss Eells?"

"Come on, I'm going to take you down to the hospital, to the emergency room. You'll be okay. Don't worry. They'll know what to do down there."

"All right," Anthony said in a dull, lifeless voice.

Miss Eells drove straight to the hospital and took Anthony into the brightly lit emergency room. A nurse told him to sit down; she'd be with him in a few minutes. He nodded dumbly and did as he was told. He felt as if he had somehow become a very small child again, fit only to be ordered around from place to place by grown-ups. Soon a doctor came. He carefully felt the two bones of Anthony's forearm. Neither of them was broken. Then his hand moved up, and Anthony winced. Hot pain shot up through his shoulder.

"So it's there, eh?" said the doctor, nodding very professionally. "Humeral fracture. We don't get many of those."

Anthony had broken the big bone of his upper arm. And what's more—as the doctor found out after he took an X-ray—the two pieces of the arm bone had separated and were now lying next to each other, like this:

The doctor thought he might have to operate to get the two pieces back where they ought to be. But first he wanted to try something else. He put Anthony's arm in a very heavy cast. Then he told him that he wanted him to spend the night in the hospital with his arm hanging down over the side of the bed. If the heavy cast did its work, the bones would slide back into place.

A few minutes later, Anthony was lying in an iron bed at the end of a long, dark hallway. His whole right arm, from fingertips to shoulder, was encased in a heavy white plaster cast. He had been given a shot of morphine to kill the pain and help him to sleep. It made him feel very relaxed and happy and drowsy. Miss Eells was sitting on a chair next to the bed. She looked at him in a kind, motherly way. There were tears in her eyes.

"I called your mother before I left the house, Anthony," Miss Eells whispered. She leaned forward and looked at his face. "But—by the way, can you still hear me?"

"Uh huh," said Anthony dreamily.

"Good. Now, I wonder if you could tell me what happened before she gets here. You don't have to if you don't want to, but I would sort of like to know."

"I was going after the treasure," said Anthony in a dull, faraway voice. "I fixed the door of Mr. Winterborn's house just like a real burglar, and then I was scared to go in, but then I thought I better try, on account of we need the money, only there was this dog and I got scared, and I tripped on a wire and fell down. I'm sorry . . . I'll . . . do . . . better . . . next . . ." Anthony's head dropped down on his shoulder. He was asleep.

I should have known he would try to burglarize that house, thought Miss Eells bitterly. *I should have known.*

But then what could she have done to stop him? Nothing, probably.

"Damn Alpheus Winterborn anyway!" said Miss Eells out loud.

A nurse at the far end of the hall heard her and turned, startled. Miss Eells's face flushed with embarrassment.

"Nice old ladies shouldn't swear," she muttered to herself as she got up to leave.

In the hall she ran into Anthony's mother. Mrs. Monday had just stepped out of the elevator, and she looked like the wrath of God. As soon as she saw Miss Eells, she lost her temper.

"What did you do to my son?" Mrs. Monday yelled. "You dragged him out in the middle of the night to go gallivanting around on some crazy scheme of yours, didn't you?"

"Easy, easy, for heaven's sake!" whispered Miss Eells. "Calm down! I didn't do anything to Anthony! He came to my house after he'd . . ." Miss Eells paused. She was on the point of telling the whole tale to Mrs. Monday, but then she changed her mind.

"Yes? After he'd what?" Mrs. Monday glared at Miss Eells impatiently.

"After he'd been out running around. I don't know why he was running around in the middle of the night. I really don't. Please believe me."

Mrs. Monday glanced around distractedly. "Well, where is he? What have they done with him?"

There was a nurse standing next to Mrs. Monday. As soon as she had heard the yelling, she had gotten up from her desk and walked over to see what was the matter. "Are you asking about Anthony Monday?" she said.

"Yes, I am. I'm his mother. Where is he?"

"He's in a bed at the end of the hall. He's asleep. His arm was set by Dr. Murphy, and he's been given a morphine injection. As far as I know, there aren't any further problems."

The nurse went on talking to Mrs. Monday. While they were talking, Miss Eells very quietly slipped away and went down the back stairs. She left the hospital by a side exit, got into her car, and drove home. When she got to her house, she went straight to her bedroom, flopped down on her bed in her clothes, and was asleep in no time.

The next morning, Anthony's mother took him home from the hospital. When he walked into his house, he found a large iron hospital bed set up for him in the parlor. There were fresh greenhouse flowers on a table in the corner, and everything had been set up to make the parlor into a bedroom for him. Doc Luescher was there, and he explained to Anthony that he would need to sleep in the hospital bed for a while, in a half-sitting-up position, because his arm still needed the pull of the heavy cast to straighten it out. The parlor had sliding doors, so the room could be made private. The doctor also explained to Anthony that he would have to exercise every day with a weight on his arm. That would help straighten it out, too.

So Anthony started on the road to recovery. It was strange sleeping in the parlor, but after a few rough nights, he got used to it. Days passed. The arm began to mend, and as it did, the bone made all sorts of funny pops and pings and twinges. Every day Anthony would spend half an hour pacing back and forth, back and forth, on the parlor rug with a pail of oranges hanging from his arm by a sling. Sometimes when he couldn't sleep at night he watched TV. All the movies seemed to be treasure movies: *The Treasure of Monte Cristo, The Return of Monte Cristo, Treasure Island*—movies like that. Sometimes, as Anthony watched these movies, a tear would come trickling down his cheek.

Anthony's mother was very nice to him and served him meals in bed. Every now and then, when they were alone together, Mrs. Monday would try to find out from Anthony just what it was that he had been doing when he broke his arm at two in the morning. Anthony didn't tell her much. He had never told her one blessed thing about the treasure of Alpheus Winterborn, and he wasn't going to start now. There was still a faint chance that someday, some way, he might get his hands on it, and then would be the time to spill the beans. He did tell his mother something, of course. He told her that on the night he broke his arm, he had been unable to sleep, so he had gotten up and wandered out into the night. He had cut across somebody's yard, and there had been this trip wire, and bingo! He had fallen down and broken his arm. He had gone to Miss Eells's house for help because it was nearby.

Mrs. Monday didn't believe a word of this tale, but she planned to worm the truth out of him when he got better.

Weeks passed, and with them, Christmas. Anthony had received some nice presents, but he wondered if he would ever get the present he longed for—from Alpheus Winterborn.

At last Anthony went back to the doctor and had the heavy cast taken off. The doctor used a little whirring electric saw to cut through the plaster shell, and when the thing came apart into two neat pieces, Anthony saw his arm again. It was a mess. It was red and puffy and covered with little curls of dead skin. Doc Luescher told him to take a good look at the arm because he wasn't going to see it again for a while. Then he began putting on the new cast, dipping long strips of elastic bandage in wet plaster and wripping them around and around Anthony's arm. The doctor X-rayed Anthony's arm again and told him that he could go back to school and even work at the library—if he was careful. Anthony was glad. He was tired of staying at home. He had learned to write fairly well with his left hand, and he had kept up with his lessons, but he really wanted to get back into the swing of things. He was bored and restless. As for the library job, he didn't know how much good a one-armed page would be at the Hoosac Public Library, but he told Miss Eells on the phone that he would do what he could.

Needless to say, Miss Eells was overjoyed that Anthony was coming back to work. She told him that he could answer the phone and stamp books with one arm. And he wouldn't have any heavy lifting to do. She said that she had missed him and that she looked forward to seeing him back on the job soon.

The very next morning, Anthony went back to school. At first he was embarrassed when everybody stared at his cast, but soon he began to be proud of it. He was like a wounded soldier. People did nice things for him, like holding doors open and getting out of the way when he went past. Miss Johansen didn't insist on neat papers from him because she knew he couldn't write very well with his left hand. She even declared a sort of holiday during the study period, and kids gathered around and signed Anthony's cast with their ballpoint pens. Naturally, everybody wanted to know how Anthony had broken his arm. But all he would say was, "Aw, I was runnin' across this yard, and I tripped." That was the only explanation that anyone was going to get from him for the time being.

Anthony still clung to the slim hope that he might yet get his hands on the treasure. For all he knew, the wood chip was still in the bolt-hole of the cellar door. At least Hugo Philpotts hadn't bought the house, as Anthony had feared. Anthony planned that when his arm was healed (the cast was due to come off in two weeks), he would have another try at burglarizing the house. But in the meantime, a Mr. Briggs Sculthorp, a lawyer who was moving to Hoosac from Mankato, had bought it. The last time Anthony passed the Winterborn house, Mr. Loomis's truck had been parked outside it again. The back of the truck had been open, and Anthony had seen, to his horror, that there were rolls of wallpaper in it!

Several times when Anthony was walking past the house, he had wanted to go around to the side to see if the wood block was still in place, but he had been afraid to look. Now, as he sat watching television with his family in the parlor on this cold, rainy winter night, he was filled with a deep feeling of foreboding. Something bad was going to happen. It was like the feeling he now got in the bone of his arm when it rained—a twinge, a kind of omen of bad luck.

The doorbell rang.

"Gee, I wonder who that is," said Anthony. The fear that had been lying in his heart all evening grew stronger.

"I'm sure I don't know," said his mother. Sighing, she got up and went to the door. It was Miss Eells. She had a wet umbrella in her hand, and a green net bag hanging from one arm. Mrs. Monday was both surprised and annoyed. Miss Eells had never come to Anthony's house before, though she had often picked him up outside in her car. "May I come in?" asked Miss Eells.

Mrs. Monday said nothing, but finally she moved aside so that Miss Eells could get past.

Miss Eells glanced uncertainly around. "Could—could I see Anthony in private for a minute or two? I have something that I want to say to him about—about our work at the library."

Again Mrs. Monday didn't answer. Instead, she turned and called into the parlor. "Anthony!"

"Yeah, Mom? What is it?"

"Miss Eells is here. She wants to talk to you."

Anthony was startled. He jumped up and ran out into the front hall.

"Hi, Anthony," said Miss Eells, smiling. "Could we talk in private for a couple of seconds? I have something I need to tell you. It won't take long."

Anthony was flustered. "Uh, sure. Mom, can we go out in the kitchen and talk?"

"I don't see why not," said Mrs. Monday. She eyed Miss Eells coldly, then turned and went back into the parlor. The sliding doors closed behind her with a loud bang.

Miss Eells followed Anthony out into the kitchen and closed the kitchen door. Then she sat down at the big round table and laid her green embroidered net bag on it. Anthony sat down, too.

"Now, then," said Miss Eells. Her face grew solemn. "Anthony," she said at last, "this evening, when I finished at the library, I dropped around at the offices of the *Daily Sentinel*. Mrs. Bump, who is a reporter there, is a friend of mine, and sometimes we sit around and have late-evening blab sessions. This evening I found her pecking away at her typewriter writing up a story. I started reading it over her shoulder, and when I found out what it was about, I asked her if I could have the carbon copy she was making. She said yes, and I brought it along with me. I think perhaps you ought to read it."

Miss Eells reached into her bag and pulled out a

sheaf of papers. They were wrinkled and spotted with rain. She pushed the papers across the table to Anthony and watched him in silence while he read.

ODD FIND MADE IN
OLD WINTERBORN HOUSE

Mr. Briggs Sculthorp of 20 Front Street, the new owner of the historic old Winterborn mansion, made a rather intriguing discovery yesterday. Workmen in the employ of Loomis and Son, painters and decorators, were stripping wallpaper in one of the upstairs back bedrooms when they noticed a large white patch in the plaster wall that they had just uncovered. At the same time, one of the workmen noticed a small "x" drawn in pencil on it. Of course, marks on old walls are common, and so are patches on plaster walls. But written across this particular patch, in small square letters, were these words: "Lucky You!" The surprised workmen immediately informed Mr. Loomis of their find, and he in turn notified Mr. Sculthorp, who decided that the matter ought to be looked into.

A chisel and a hammer were procured, and it was short work to hack away the plaster under the spot where the rather tantalizing message had been scrawled. Within the wall, resting on a wooden brace, was a small black metal cash box of a sort that was in use in offices and stores about fifty years ago. Mr. Sculthorp, who was present when this find was made, was understandably quite excited. One can imagine his surprise when the box was opened and within it was discovered only a small envelope, yellowed with age.

The workmen crowded around, and everyone held his breath. The gum on the flap of the envelope still held tight, so Mr. Sculthorp took a penknife from his pocket and slit the envelope open. He then shook the contents out into his hand. Groans of disappointment went up from the workmen and Mr. Loomis. In Mr. Sculthorp's outstretched hand lay the withered remains of a four-leaf clover. . . .

"I'm sorry, Anthony," said Miss Eells, "I really, truly am. There's no one in the world I would rather see get rich than you. But I was afraid it would end this way."

Anthony was crushed. He sat clenching the paper in his hands. He stared at the typed words that writhed and squirmed before his eyes. This was the end. This was the end of everything.

"As soon as I found out about this, I decided to come over and tell you the news myself," Miss Eells went on gently, "because I didn't want you to just stumble upon this piece all of a sudden, by yourself."

Anthony clenched the paper tighter. He stared hard at the wall. His lower lip quivered, and his eyes filled with tears. "God . . . damn old Alpheus Winterborn!" he said in a shaking voice.

"Go ahead," said Miss Eells. "Damn him all you want. He has it coming. And tear up the article if it'll make you feel any better. I don't need it any more."

Anthony tore the papers in his hands to shreds, and he tore the shreds to bits. Then he put his hands to his face and sobbed bitterly. Miss Eells watched him silently. When he was done, he just sat there, staring desolately at the table that was covered with the shreds of torn paper. Miss Eells tried to talk to him, but he wouldn't answer. Finally she got up, sighed, picked up her bag, and went out to the front hall. The front door opened and closed quietly. Miss Eells was gone.

Later, when Anthony had pulled himself together,

he gathered up the torn bits of paper and threw them into a wastebasket. Then he blew his nose a few times and went back to the parlor. In the dark, no one noticed that his eyes were red from crying.

"Well, what was *that* all about?" said his mother from the other side of the room.

"Nothin', Ma," muttered Anthony. "Miss Eells just wanted me to do something for her."

"Seems like kind of a production over nothing," Mrs. Monday grumbled. "Doesn't she know that on Sunday evenings people like to be alone with their families?"

Anthony said nothing, but a small shudder passed through his body. He could imagine what his mother would say if she ever found out what a sucker he had been. He could hear the words clearly in his mind, as if his mother were saying them out loud: *The trouble with you, Anthony, is that you're gullible, and you're lazy. You think that things are going to be handed to you on a silver platter. Well, they aren't. No one's going to hand you a million dollars. You have to work for what you get in this world.*

The trouble was that Anthony felt he *had* worked. He had sweated and slaved over that dumb poem. He had planned and plotted and schemed, and all he had to show for it was a broken arm. When the TV show was over, he went upstairs to his room and sat at his desk for a while, staring out into the rainy darkness. Then he opened up the black binder with Alpheus Winterborn's message in it and tore out all the sheets. He tore them up and threw them in the wastebasket, and he pitched the empty binder into a corner. Then he cried a little more and went to bed. As he pulled the covers up around himself and settled down to sleep, he said to himself, *Well, anyway, it's all over with.*

About that, however, he was wrong.

Chapter 11

I t snowed a lot that winter in Minnesota, especially up north. Pictures of the heavy snowfall were printed in the *Hoosac Daily Sentinel*. They were sent down by wire from cities like Hibbing and St. Cloud and Bemidji and Duluth. The pictures showed mountainous drifts piled by the roadsides and houses buried up to the second-story windows in snow. Many people predicted that there would be floods along the Mississippi when all that snow started to melt. But the people of Hoosac felt safe. The town had been flooded in the past, but there hadn't been a really serious flood since 1915, and no one really expected one now.

Early in January, Mr. Monday had gone back to work. He had a Grand Reopening party and served Christmas punch to all his old patrons. At the party he introduced his new assistant, the man who would do all the lifting and carrying for him—Charley Odegard, the twenty-year-old son of the man who owned the building in which Mr. Monday's saloon was housed. Charley told the patrons of Monday's Cigar Store that he'd do his best, and Mr. Monday said he was proud to have Charley on his team, and everybody cheered and gave Charley a round of applause. Mr. Monday had a great time at his own party. He felt cheerful and healthy for the first time since he had had his first heart attack way back in August. He said he felt great, and then everybody cheered and sang "For He's a Jolly Good Fellow" and other songs. It was a really fine party.

Needless to say, Mrs. Monday was delighted that her husband was back at work. So were Anthony and Keith. It meant the end of worry and despair. Business was booming. Money was coming in. Now the treasure of Alpheus Winterborn didn't matter so much. Of course, Anthony still thought about the treasure—he couldn't help it. But he thought about the treasure the way you think about somebody you used to know who was dead. In a funny way, Anthony was glad the treasure hunt was over. It had taken up an awful lot of his time. Now he felt as if a weight had been lifted from his shoulders. Everything was going along great. Everything would be all right.

One morning in March, Anthony was out in the front hall putting on his jacket and his cap. He was getting ready to go to school. Suddenly the mail slot flapped, and a bundle of letters came sliding in. He bent over to pick them up, and he noticed that the one on top was addressed to him. The return address showed that the letter was from the First National Bank of Hoosac, and the letter was stamped "Personal and Confidential." Suddenly Anthony felt very frightened. He glanced over his shoulder to see if his mother was around, then stuffed the letter into his pants pocket. Halfway to school, he stopped and pulled out the letter. He ripped open the envelope and pulled out a note. It was dated the day before and it said:

Dear Mr. Monday:

A matter of some importance has come to my attention, and it requires that you and I have a small consultation. It concerns your account at this bank and a minor irregularity that needs straightening out. Will you be so good as to come to my office after school at 3:30 on Tuesday, the twelfth of March? The bank will, of course, be closed at that time, but I have instructed the guard to let you in when you knock. It is important that you keep this appointment and that you come in person. Don't be late.

Sincerely yours,
HUGO C. PHILPOTTS

First Vice-President,
The First National Bank
of Hoosac, Minnesota

P.S.: It is not necessary for either of your parents to accompany you. The papers requiring your signature may be countersigned later, at your parents' convenience.

As Anthony read this note, he felt a vague, formless fear growing in his mind. He didn't know much about the world of high finance, but he didn't think that a big shot like Mr. Philpotts would be likely to be sending him notes about his savings account. That was the sort of thing that his employees would take care of. Anthony folded up the note and stuck it back in his pocket.

There was a troubled look on his face. He decided that before he went to see Mr. Philpotts, he would have to show this note to Miss Eells.

After school, Anthony marched straight over to the library to Miss Eells's office. He pulled the note out of his pocket and shoved it across the desk to Miss Eells. She opened it and read it, and as she read, her eyebrows rose, and a little surprised smile appeared on her face. Then she frowned.

"Well!" she said as she folded the note back up. "If that isn't the darndest!"

"Do you—do you think it's anything bad, Miss Eells?" asked Anthony anxiously.

Miss Eells took her glasses off and stared at the wall. "I don't know. I'm sure that if you were to show up at the bank with your mother, he'd produce some sort of falderal for you to sign, and that would be the end of it —for the time being. By the way, did you tell your mother that you got this note?"

Anthony shook his head. "Nope. I was scared to."

Miss Eells put her glasses back on. "You know, there may be reason for you to be scared. I don't want to alarm you, but it seems to me that there is more in this note than meets the eye. I think it was good that you didn't tell your mother. It says here that he wants to see you today at three-thirty. That's fifteen minutes from now. Are you going to see him?"

"Yeah. I guess I have to, unless you think I shouldn't go."

Miss Eells drummed her fingers on the desk. "Oh, I think you ought to go," she said at last. "There's no doubt in my mind about that. And as soon as you find out what he's got up his sleeve, come back and tell me, will you?"

Anthony grinned. "Sure," he said. He was glad at times like this that he had Miss Eells on his side. Very glad.

A few minutes later, Anthony found himself standing outside the front door of the First National Bank of Hoosac. The door was made of glass, and through it Anthony could see people working inside the bank, even though the door was locked and the regular business day was over. A guard in a blue uniform stood just inside. Anthony rapped on the glass, and the man let him in.

"Are you Anthony Monday?" he asked.

"Yeah, that's me."

"Well, you're to go to Mr. Philpotts's office. It's down at the end of that corridor. The third door on your left. His name is on the glass. You can't miss it."

"Thanks."

Anthony walked down the corridor and stopped outside a door with a frosted glass pane set in it. The gold letters on the pane said HUGO C. PHILPOTTS, *Vice-President*. Anthony knocked and waited for a response. After a few minutes, he heard footsteps and saw a shadow moving behind the glass. The door opened.

"Hello, young man. How are you today?" Hugo Philpotts smiled stiffly and bowed. He stepped aside and waved Anthony in.

"Okay, I guess."

Anthony walked in, and Mr. Philpotts closed the door. "This way, young man." Anthony followed Mr. Philpotts across a little bare room that had a filing cabinet, a desk, and two chairs in it. There was no one sitting at the desk. As they passed the desk, Mr. Philpotts tapped it and said, "This is my secretary's desk. I sent her home early because I want our conversation to be private. She has a bad habit of listening in on the intercom." He

107

laughed a small, cold, mirthless laugh. Then he pushed open another door, a big, stout oak-paneled door, marked "Private." Inside was a comfortable-looking office. There was a large walnut desk with a green marble inkstand on it. The carpet was wine-colored and very thick, and all the walls were covered with panels of dark, polished wood. Heavy red draperies hung over all the windows, shutting out the sunlight. A floor lamp burned next to the desk. It cast a pool of quiet light over the desk and the carpet.

Anthony followed Hugo Philpotts across the carpet. At one corner of the desk was an easy chair for visitors to sit in, and next to the easy chair was a bronze ash tray on a fluted stand. Behind the desk was Hugo Philpotts's own chair. It had red damask upholstery and tall, twisty wooden pillars running up the sides. The back of the chair was very high, and at the top was a wooden coat of arms. Anthony thought the chair looked like a throne. And behind the chair, up on the wall, was a portrait. It was lit by a green-shaded lamp that hung out over the top of the frame. It was a portrait of Alpheus Winterborn.

"Do sit down," said Hugo Philpotts, patting the back of the easy chair.

Anthony sat down, and as he sank into the seat, the green leather cushion under him hissed like an inner tube. Hugo Philpotts went around behind the desk and sat down on the throne chair. He folded his hands on the desk and stared hard at Anthony. There was a cold smirk on his thin, whitish lips. One corner of his moustache twitched nervously. His manner so far had been courteous—in a greasy, oily way—but it was plain to Anthony that Mr. Philpotts had something besides savings accounts on his mind.

"Now then, young man," said Hugo Philpotts, as he rubbed his hands together, "you have probably guessed that I didn't ask you here so that we could talk about your savings account. I suppose that by rights I ought to have asked Miss Eells to come here, but I decided that I'd approach her through you. I'm sure that by the time I'm finished talking with you, you'll want very much to help me. You'll want to beg her and plead with her to give me what I want. And as soon as she finds out how things stand, I'm sure she will be cooperative. She likes you very much. Everyone knows that." Hugo coughed, and Anthony stared at him.

"But why be mysterious?" Hugo Philpotts went on as he stroked his moustache with his forefinger. "I'm sure you hate beating around the bush as much as I do, so I'll come right to the point. That Eells woman has something that is rightfully mine, and I want you to make her give it to me. What I mean is, I want what was in the envelope, or bag, or box, or whatever it was that was glued to the back of the mirror that Miss Eells bought at that auction out in Rolling Stone. I want it, and I want it *now*." He rapped his knuckles on the desk.

Anthony was stunned. He couldn't have been more surprised if Hugo had asked him for the moon. All along, Anthony had wondered if this mysterious meeting had something to do with Alpheus Winterborn's treasure. Miss Eells hadn't said so in so many words, but it was obvious that she thought the treasure was at the bottom of the mystery, too. Both Anthony and Miss Eells felt sure that Hugo had stolen the mirror, but Anthony had never, in his wildest dreams, expected to hear Hugo himself own up to the theft. That, however, was what he had just done.

Hugo saw how surprised Anthony was, and this seemed

to amuse him. He laughed harshly. "Surprised, aren't you? Here I am, telling you right out in the open that I stole that ridiculous mirror. Naughty of me, wasn't it? Would you like to call up the police and tell them all about it?" He shoved the telephone across the desk toward Anthony.

Anthony sat there with his mouth open. Then suddenly anger flared up inside him. "You're darn right I will!" he said, and he jumped to his feet. But as he reached for the phone, Hugo clamped his hand down over the receiver.

"Not so fast, young man. Not so fast. You don't know what you're doing. In the first place, I merely took back what was rightfully mine. I won that mirror, fair and square, at the auction. If that old crook of an auctioneer hadn't cheated me, I wouldn't have had to steal it to get it. And in the second place, if you say one word to anyone about what I did, you'll be getting your father into a very great deal of trouble."

Anthony froze. "My father?" He slowly sank back into his seat.

"That's better," said Hugo, smiling maliciously. He took his hand off the phone, but he continued to stare hard at Anthony. "I'm sure you don't want any trouble. Nobody likes trouble. And you'll be saving yourself and Miss Eells and your father a great deal of trouble if you'll just go along like a good boy and help me get what I want."

Anthony felt very confused. The threat against his father had come totally out of the blue. And why on earth did Mr. Philpotts want the envelope with the clue in it? It was a clue to a treasure that didn't exist. It was like asking for the key to a house that had been torn down. It didn't make any sense.

Anthony shifted nervously in his seat. "M-Mr. Philpotts," he stammered, "all this kind of . . . well, it sounds kind of nutty to me. I don't see why you want—"

Hugo cut him off. "So it sounds nutty, does it? Well, it will all seem very clear and sane in a couple of minutes. But first I want to tell you that I've had my eye on you for some time. I've been watching you ever since you slid Alpheus Winterborn's lucky piece across the counter to me."

Anthony's mouth dropped open.

"Oh, yes. My Uncle Alpheus used to carry a ten-dollar gold piece around with him. When I was a child, he would let me play with it now and then, and I have always remembered that there were two notches on the nose of the Liberty head on one side. He made them with his jackknife. When I saw those notches, I was suspicious, and then, just to be absolutely certain, I took the coin into the back room and examined it with a magnifying glass. Sure enough, there under the eagle on the other side were Uncle Alpheus's initials. The letters were very small—I think he had them engraved by a jeweler—but they were there, and that proved to me beyond a shadow of a doubt that the coin was his. And then I thought to myself, what is this boy doing with Alpheus Winterborn's lucky piece? Where did he get it? Of course, I said to myself, this boy works at the library, doesn't he? He said he did and that Miss Eells had sent him down with the coin. Maybe Alpheus dropped it in some dusty corner of the library when he was living there in the months just before his death, and then this boy found it. That seemed reasonable.

"But I still felt there might be more to all this. So I kept my eye on you, until we met at that auction out in Rolling Stone—when your friend Miss Eells and I both wanted the same thing, and by cheating she managed to get it. I said to myself, something is up. First the coin, and now this mirror. Both of them belonged to Alpheus Winterborn. Now suppose, I said to myself, just suppose that boy found a message of some kind with that coin."

Anthony squirmed. Hugo Philpotts's guess was uncomfortably close to the truth.

"You see," Hugo continued, leaning back in his chair and lighting a cigarette, "my Uncle Alpheus was a strange man. He liked to hide things, and he liked to drop hints. Sly little hints. He used to have dinner over at our house during the years when the library was being built, and he dropped hints now and then about a valuable object, or collection of objects, that he had hidden somewhere. He wouldn't say what this little treasure was, but my mother and I gathered that it was something really wonderful, something worth maybe hundreds of thousands of dollars. Well, naturally, I wondered what the treasure could be, and—more important—I wondered *where* it could be. I tried on more than one occasion to worm the truth out of my dear old uncle, but he was a close-mouthed old—uh, gentleman, and whenever I brought the treasure up, he would shut his mouth tighter than a clam."

Hugo Philpotts paused to flick the ash off his cigarette. Then he went on. "In all the years that have passed since my Uncle Alpheus died, I've thought a great deal about this real or imaginary treasure. Naturally, I tried at first to convince myself that Uncle Alpheus had been putting me on. He was well known as a practical joker in his time, after all. But over the years I became thoroughly convinced that there really was a Winterborn treasure of some sort hidden away in or near the town

112

of Hoosac. Jewels, maybe. A diamond necklace, or rubies or emeralds. Rare coins, or stamps perhaps." He suddenly looked up at Anthony. "Which was it, by the way? Which of my guesses was correct?"

Anthony blinked. "Huh?"

Hugo Philpotts ground out his cigarette with an abrupt, angry motion and leaned forward in his chair. "Oh, don't play games with me, child! There was a treasure hidden in the back of that mirror, wasn't there? Well, wasn't there?"

So that was it. Hugo thought that the treasure had been in the mirror!

"Mr. Philpotts, I think you got the wrong idea. There wasn't any—"

"So you're going to play dumb, are you? Do you have any idea how stupid and idiotic your lying is? I can see through you, I can read you like a book! And anyway, do you take me for a fool? I saw the glue spot—I could tell there was something there once! Well, what was it? Are you going to tell me?" Hugo's face was getting red. His shoulders were hunched, his hands tightly clenched. He was waiting for an answer.

Anthony felt as if he were losing his mind. "Mr. Philpotts," he began, "y-you got it all wrong. There—there wasn't anything inside that old mirror except just a note that said that there was a treasure inside Mr. Winterborn's house. But there wasn't anything there, just that old tin box with a four-leaf clover inside of it, like it said in the papers. Didn't you read about it when they found that box?"

Hugo Philpotts stared at Anthony. He drummed his fingers on the desk top. He seemed to be considering. "Oh, I see it all now," he said in a low voice. "You and that Eells woman read about that silly box and figured you could put me off the track that way. Well, it won't work. Of course I read about the box. It was just one of Uncle Alpheus's practical jokes, that's all it was. But that doesn't alter the fact that you and that woman are trying to hide the real treasure from me."

"But Mr. Winter—uh, I mean, Mr. Philpotts—I keep telling you there *isn't* any treasure, there was just that crummy old—"

"All right," said Hugo Philpotts. His voice was calm now, but there was a malicious gleam in his eye. "Since you're going to be uncooperative, I'll have to be a bit more persuasive." He shoved his desk chair back, got up, and walked over to a steel filing cabinet that stood in a corner of the room. From one of the drawers he reached in and pulled out a manila folder. Then he walked back to his desk, sat down, and opened up the folder. "Do you know that your father doesn't own the building where he operates his, uh, 'business'? Do you know that? Eh?"

Anthony felt a hard knot forming in the pit of his stomach. "Yeah, I know."

Hugo gave Anthony a contemptuous look. "Well, then, you must realize that if the person who does own the building decides not to renew your father's lease— which, I think, comes up for renewal in about a week— then your father will have to get *out*. It would be very sad if that happened, especially since your father has had a heart attack. No, it's two, isn't it? Two heart attacks. Well, now, I wouldn't be a bit surprised if your father's heart were permanently weakened, and if he got a bad piece of news, the shock might kill him. Wouldn't you say that was likely?"

Anthony said nothing. He was thoroughly scared, but he also felt defiant. This rotten man was threatening to

114

hurt his father. But how could he do that? Mr. Odegard, the guy who owned the building, was an old pal of Mr. Monday's, and Mr. Monday had just hired his son to help him at the saloon. It didn't seem very likely that Mr. Odegard would throw his father out.

"You can't make Mr. Odegard toss my dad out of his store," said Anthony in a trembling, angry voice. "He wouldn't ever do that! Not ever!"

"Oh, he has no choice in the matter any more," said Mr. Philpotts coolly. "You see, Magnus Odegard has just gone bankrupt. The matter hasn't been made public yet, but the fact is that he's broke. Well, it so happens that all his assets—his stocks and bonds, and the buildings he owns, and so on—have become the property of the bank. *This* bank." Mr. Philpotts paused. He leafed through the papers in the folder that lay before him. Finally, he pulled out a very official-looking document with a gold paper seal at the bottom. The Old English letters at the top of the paper said "Deed." Mr. Philpotts held the document up for Anthony to see. "This is the deed to the property at 412 Minnesota Avenue, where Monday's Cigar Store is located. The building is in a good location—excellent for the kind of business that your father is engaged in. What do you suppose would happen if the bank decided to tear this building down for a parking lot? Or give the lease to somebody else? What do you suppose would happen to your father's weak heart? Eh? *Just what do you suppose would happen?*"

Chapter **12**

Hugo Philpotts glared stonily at Anthony. He held up three fingers of his right hand. "Three days," he said. "Three days is what I'll give you, my dear boy. And that's *all* I'll give you. After that, your father will have to set up his business in a tent somewhere. You go back to Miss Eells and tell her what I've said. Tell her I mean *business*!" He reached into his vest pocket and pulled out a watch. "And now I see that I have to be on my way if I'm going to catch my train to Minneapolis. Good day, young man. You may leave. The guard will let you out."

Anthony got up and stumbled out of Hugo Philpotts's office. He went straight back to the library and told Miss Eells everything that had happened. She was shocked, and she was angry. It had been bad enough that Hugo had burglarized her house and given her a bump on the head. Now he was trying to twist poor Anthony's arm, and all to get his hands on a treasure that wasn't there! Anthony was in a terrible state. He just sat in a chair in Miss Eells's office, shaking his head and saying, "Gosh, I just can't believe it, I just can't believe it!" over and over again.

"Isn't there *anything* we can do, Miss Eells?" he said at last.

"I don't know. I'll go and see him, Maybe I can pound some sense into his head. I'll try to reason with him," said Miss Eells.

"You can't!" Anthony wailed. "He's gone up to Minneapolis on the train!"

Outside the windows of the library something ominous was happening. The river was rising. All the snow that had fallen during the winter was melting now. And it had been raining for a solid two weeks, almost without a letup. The river looked swollen, and a lot of the low-lying areas outside the town had already been flooded. Men were laying sandbags on the levees, the high earthen banks that had been built at various points along the river side of the town. Still, nobody thought that a flood was coming. The sandbags were simply there "in case." But there was no danger. No need to worry—or so most people said.

If there is anything worse than having something bad happen, it is *waiting* for something bad to happen. Anthony was in a constant state of torment now. Whenever he was at home and the phone rang, he jumped. At the dinner table, he glanced furtively at his mother, wondering if she suspected anything. If she did, she gave no sign. Mr. Monday was very cheerful. He whistled and hummed and sang when he was around the house and talked about how good business was. All this light-heartedness just made Anthony feel worse. He couldn't help imagining how his dad would feel when he found out that his store was being sold out from under him.

If only he hadn't gone poking around finding notes, Anthony thought. If only he hadn't pestered Miss Eells into bidding on that old mirror. If only he hadn't had all these silly ideas of getting rich quick.

Wednesday passed. Thursday morning dawned. Time was hurtling on, speeding on, seconds and minutes whipping past. When Anthony showed up for work at the library on Thursday, he had one faint hope left. Maybe somewhere, hidden in the library, there was a clue to the *real* treasure. Anthony knew he was grasping at straws, but as soon as he had checked in with Miss Eells, he went straight to the upstairs reading room and started taking books down. All books in this room were books that Alpheus Winterborn had owned. Maybe inside one of them would be a clue of some kind. One after another, Anthony opened books, leafed through them in great haste, and then shut them. Open, look, slam, open, look, slam, over and over and over and over. Clouds of dust rose, and Anthony started sneezing. Sweat was pouring down his face. Still he went on. As he leafed through the books, he noticed that all of them had bookplates. Alpheus Winterborn's personal book-plate was interesting: It showed a clown in a clown suit that was divided right down the middle. Half was red and half was black. Even the big puffy pompons that served as buttons for the suit were divided this way. Under the figure of the clown was a scroll, and—not surprisingly—these words were on it: BELIEVE ONLY HALF

118

OF WHAT YOU READ. It was the same motto that was on that silly half-moon where Anthony had found the message. And it was the same one that was on the stone carving over the front door of the library. It was a crazy motto. What the heck did it mean, anyway? Anthony imagined somebody reading only half of every book that came into his hands, or half of every page, or half of every poem . . .

Anthony paused. He was standing on the stepladder with one of Alpheus Winterborn's books open in his hand. There was a curious look on his face. He had almost had a thought, but it had gotten away from him. There's nothing more maddening than having some idea *almost* form itself in your mind and then zip away while you're trying to get hold of it. It's like almost remembering somebody's name, or almost remembering something very important that you're supposed to do. Anthony stood there chewing his lip and trying to remember. What was it that had popped into his mind and then popped right out again? He thought and thought, but whatever it was, he couldn't bring it back.

Finally, he gave up. He looked at his blackened hands and the pile of books on the stepladder in front of him, and he decided that he'd been wasting his time. There were no clues there.

But what *was* it that had been in the back of his mind? It had something to do with Alpheus Winterborn's motto, but what? Oh, well. No use. It was really gone now. Gone for good.

It rained all morning, and on into the afternoon. The wind began to blow, and the rain swept past in sheets. It spattered loudly against the windows, and the panes rattled and shook. After lunch, Anthony was in the West Reading Room putting some books on the shelves.

119

Through the wide arch that opened into the center section of the library, Anthony could see Miss Eells sitting at the circulation desk. She had one of the drawers from the card catalog in front of her. The long metal rod that held the cards in place had been pulled out, and the cards lay loose on the desk top in front of her. There was no one in the library but the two of them.

Anthony gazed gratefully for a while at Miss Eells. Miss Eells was a good friend to him. He knew that. Whatever happened now, he was glad she was on his side.

A gust of wind hit the window behind Anthony. The glass rattled violently.

"Gee," called Anthony. "It's really blowing out there, isn't it?"

"Yes," answered Miss Eells without looking up. "It's blowing up a storm. There's a real doozer predicted for tonight. Thunder, lightning—the whole works. And the river's still rising. It's up above flood crest. In fact, they say it'd be pouring into the town right now if it weren't for those men out there laying sandbags."

Anthony had never been in a flood before, though he had read about them. "What would happen if the water got in past the sandbags?" he asked.

"Lots of things. The river water is polluted, and it would pour into the wells that a lot of people in Hoosac get their water from. That would really mess things up. It would start pouring into the basements, and what with all the mud and silt and stuff, there'd be a filthy mess to clean up afterward. I've got some men coming in later this afternoon to move the magazines up from the basement storage room, just in case. Ugh! Can you imagine what it would be like, sorting through a lot of soggy magazines?" Miss Eells made a face. It was a pretty repulsive thought.

"Could anybody get killed?" Anthony asked.

Miss Eells thought a minute. "Probably not. Not in the kind of flood we're likely to have. Of course, it *could* happen. But let's hope that nobody in Hoosac gets himself into that kind of fix."

Another strong gust hit the window behind Anthony. He turned around and looked out. The bare branches heaved and tossed. They bent under the lash of wind and rain. In the distance, Anthony could see men laying sandbags on top of the stone wall that gave Levee Park its name. Then he happened to glance up at the bronze reindeer that stood at the top of the tower. He blinked and stared again. All this wind, and the reindeer wasn't moving!

"Hey, Miss Eells, I think the weather vane is stuck!" Anthony called out.

Miss Eells sighed. "Of course it is. Haven't you ever noticed that before? It doesn't work. Never has—it's jammed somehow. I don't know what's wrong with it. Needs grease, maybe."

Anthony turned and looked up at the reindeer again. Now, once more, something was stirring in his mind. What was it? He began to wonder if he were losing his marbles. Then he shrugged. Whatever it was, it was gone, like that thought he had almost had in the upstairs reading room.

The library closed at five on Thursday. Miss Eells offered to drive Anthony home because of the bad weather, and he gladly accepted her offer. On the way, Miss Eells turned on her car radio. She had barely flipped the button when, through the crackle of the static, came a voice saying, ". . . a condition of emergency has been declared for the city of Hoosac and surrounding areas. As a precautionary measure, the lower end of town, from Division Street to Walnut, will be evacuated . . ."

"Hey, that's us!" said Anthony excitedly.

"Sshhh! Listen!"

There was another storm of static, and then the voice went on. ". . . will be able to take refuge at Immaculate Conception Academy on Academy Boulevard. Work is already underway to convert the classrooms there into temporary shelters for those living in the low-lying parts of town. I repeat, there is no need for alarm. This is merely a precautionary measure. I also repeat, it would be inadvisable to attempt to leave the town by way of the bridges and causeways. Many of the low-lying areas around Hoosac are already flooded, and roads are under water in many places. It would be wise to bring up from basements any—"

Miss Eells snapped the radio off. "Wow! It sounds like we're in for it, eh, Anthony?"

"Yeah, I guess so. I wish the flood would wash old Hugo Philpotts out to sea."

Miss Eells smiled wryly. "That would be nice, wouldn't it? Well, here's your house. I guess I'll be seeing you up at the academy tonight. Come to think of it, I'd better follow that guy's advice and bring some stuff up out of my basement. I'd hate to have all my peach preserves ruined by that filthy river water."

"G'bye, Miss Eells," said Anthony as he got out of the car. "See you later."

It was an exciting night in the town of Hoosac. The National Guard units were called out, and khaki-colored trucks and jeeps rumbled through the streets. The guardsmen were there to direct the people who were being evacuated and to prevent looting. They wore brown uniforms and brown helmets, and they carried rifles with bayonets on the end of them. Sound trucks rolled up

122

and down the streets of Hoosac blaring instructions. Then the electrical storm hit. Thunder rumbled and lightning flashed, and more rain came pelting down. Police cars roared past Anthony's house, sirens screaming and blue lights flashing.

Inside the Monday home, things were at sixes and sevens. Everybody was doing something—rushing here, rushing there, unplugging lights, turning off the furnace, checking this, checking that, getting ready for the flood. Mrs. Monday packed some suitcases and made some sandwiches in case there wasn't anything to eat up at the academy. Mr. Monday went down to the basement and helped Keith and Anthony bring newspapers and jars of pickled fruit up to the kitchen. Mrs. Monday had warned her husband not to work too hard on account of his bad heart, but he pitched in and helped anyway.

About eight o'clock that evening, Anthony was in his room packing his own small suitcase. He felt excited, the way people often do when there is a crisis of some kind—war or hurricane or tornado or flood. Outside, sirens wailed and sound trucks blared. Thunder rolled, and from his window Anthony could see lightning flashing fitfully, lighting up jagged cloud banks for brief seconds. A long line of cars was moving past the house. The red reflections of their taillights stained the streets. On the corner was a police car with a flashing blue light, and Anthony could see a policeman in a yellow slicker waving a flashlight with a red plastic cone on the end of it.

"Anthony, are you getting packed, or are you daydreaming as usual?" his mother called.

"I'm packing, Ma!" Anthony turned away from the window and started throwing clothes into his suitcase. He often daydreamed when he was doing something like drying the dishes or stacking books at the library. It was a habit of his. Now, although he was excited and was supposed to be hurrying, he drifted off again. All sorts of odd images came to his mind. He thought about the stuck weather vane and the reindeer on top of the tower. He thought about that mocking, grinning half-moon on the front of the library, and the sign underneath that said BELIEVE ONLY HALF OF WHAT YOU READ.

All of a sudden, for no reason at all, everything came together in his mind. The things he had been trying to make sense of all day suddenly *did* make sense. His face lit up. He knew now. As if by magic, *he knew*. He knew where the real treasure of Alpheus Winterborn was!

Chapter 13

ANTHONY was so excited that he felt as if he were going to jump right out of his skin. He wanted to run up and down the room screaming at the top of his voice, but he was afraid that his folks would think he had lost his mind. So he kept his screams in and stood there, tense, clenching his fists. His face felt flushed, and his ears burned. What should he do? Well, emergency or no emergency, flood or no flood, he had to call up Miss Eells and tell her. He simply *had* to.

Down the stairs Anthony ran. He picked up the phone and asked for the operator and gave her Miss Eells's number. Fortunately, Keith and his folks were still busy upstairs packing. They didn't know that he was downstairs on the phone. Not that it would have made any difference to Anthony at this point—he would have called Miss Eells even if the whole town had been standing around listening.

"Hello?"

"Hey, Miss Eells! Boy, am I glad to hear your voice!" he fairly shouted. "It's me, Anthony!"

There were a lot of crackling sounds on the telephone line, like those lightning sometimes causes. For a moment Anthony thought he heard another voice, but then Miss Eells shouted into his ear, "Good grief, Anthony! What's the matter? What's happened?"

In a breathless voice, Anthony told Miss Eells where he thought the treasure was, and he explained how he had figured it all out.

"Good heavens! Well, you know you may be onto something! I won't guarantee it because there has already been a false lead in this treasure hunt, as you very well know. But I must say, it's a very ingenious guess. Congratulations!"

"What do you think, Miss Eells? Do you think we should go down and get it out now? Huh?"

"Oh, I don't know about that. It's been there for quite a few years now, and it can stay there a little longer. If it's there. I would suggest that we wait till this ridiculous flood crisis is over with."

"Are you sure? You don't think somebody else might grab it before we do?"

"Not a chance. Nobody else besides us is looking for the treasure except Hugo Philpotts, and he thinks it was in that stupid mirror. Look, Anthony, I'd love to go on chatting, but I've got to go pack and do some other things before I leave. I'll see you up at the academy."

"Okay, Miss Eells. Hey! I just had a great idea!"

"You seem to be full of them this evening. What is it?"

"Why don't you bring your chess set and meet me somewhere so we can play a game while we're waiting to see if there's going to be a flood or not? How about it, huh?"

"Hmm—sounds like a good plan to me. Why not? Okay, I'll pack my set, and—tell you what, I'll meet you at the main entrance of the classroom building of the academy. Where the pillars are. Do you know where I mean?"

Anthony thought a minute. "Yeah, I guess I do. All right, Miss Eells, I'll meet you there by the pillars. When do you think you'll get there?"

"No telling exactly. I have to finish up a few things here first. I'll see you when I see you, as my father used to say. So long now, and keep dry."

"G'bye, Miss Eells."

Anthony hung up the phone. He stood there a moment thinking about the treasure. He had half a mind to ignore Miss Eells's advice and run down right away and dig the treasure out. But at this point, Anthony's mother came charging down the stairs with a suitcase in her hand.

"Anthony Monday! What on earth are you doing standing there with that foolish look on your face? Is your bag packed?"

"Uh huh. I'm all ready to go, Mom."

"Well, you don't look like it. Haven't you got any sense, Anthony? Go get your bag and take it to the car! Hurry up! Get a move on, for heaven's sake!"

"Okay, Mom." Anthony dashed up the stairs and got his bag. A few minutes later he was in the back seat of the car with Keith. His mom was in front, and his dad was driving. They pulled out of the driveway and joined the long line of cars that was creeping slowly through the streets in the pouring rain. As they drove, Anthony saw soldiers standing on the sidewalks. They were using walkie-talkies. At one corner he saw a jeep pulled up on a lawn. Two helmeted guardsmen sat in it, watching the long procession of cars crawl past. Rain beat on the roof of the car. The Mondays moved on at a snail's pace, staying just a few feet behind the car in front of them. Anthony saw a long double row of taillights ahead of him. It was crawling slowly up the hill, heading for the high ground, for the academy.

Immaculate Conception Academy was a Catholic girls' school. The girls had already been sent home for their Easter vacation. Now nuns and volunteer workers were busy making beds and hanging up sheets to divide the bigger rooms up into smaller ones so that people could sleep and have a little privacy. But everybody hoped that it wouldn't be necessary for the people from the lower part of town to spend the night there. With luck, the walls of sandbags would hold, and the refugees would be able to go back to their homes before morning. But the river was still rising, and rain was coming down in buckets. No one really knew what was going to happen.

Around nine o'clock in the evening, the Mondays' car pulled into a parking lot out behind the main classroom building of the academy. A policeman stood nearby, waving the traffic on. He wore a wet black slicker with a white stripe across it, and he was waving a flashlight. Rain dripped from the peak of his cap. Mr. Monday nosed the car into a parking place. With their baggage, the Mondays trotted up the walk to the back entrance of the main classroom building. Inside was a policeman with a bullhorn who told them to go up to the third floor. The marble stairs were wet and slippery because men in galoshes had been marching up and down them. The Mondays walked down a long, dark corridor and stopped outside a lighted room. Inside, mattresses had been laid out on the floor. A coffee urn steamed in one corner, and there was a steel cart loaded with sandwiches and other goodies. A nun in a long black habit was there to meet them.

"Hello. I'm Sister Louisa. This is where you'll be staying. And your name is . . . ?"

"Monday," said Anthony's dad. "I'm Howard Monday, and this is my wife, and these are my sons, Keith and Anthony. It's real nice of you folks to set things up this way."

The nun smiled. "Thank you. We hope you will be able to return to your home before long, but if not, this place is yours to stay in as long as you like. Make yourself comfortable."

The Mondays put down their suitcases and sat on some chairs that were arranged nearby. The mattresses had clean sheets and blankets on them, but nobody thought about sleeping. It was only a little after nine, and they were all terribly excited. Mr. Monday wandered out into the hall and started talking to a friend of his he had seen passing by. Mrs. Monday got out her knitting, and Keith started reading a book. Anthony was all at loose ends. He began pacing up and down, glancing at his watch from time to time. He was eager for Miss Eells to get there. She had told him that she would meet him at the main entrance of the academy as soon as she got settled. Had she arrived yet? There was no way of knowing. There were two big dormitories with hundreds of rooms in them, and there was this building. She could be anywhere.

"Mom," Anthony said after a while, "could I go downstairs and look around? I won't go away. I'll just stay near the building."

Mrs. Monday looked up. "Oh, I guess so. But don't get in the way of the policemen. They have a job to do, you know. And be back in half an hour. Do you understand?"

"Sure, Mom. I will. G'bye."

Anthony put on his raincoat and rain hat and walked down the long, dark corridor and two flights of stairs. On the first floor, there were lots of people milling around and talking. Anthony slipped through the crowd, and before long he found himself out in front of the building under the tall, pillared porch. Below him lay the town. There were lights on here and there, but most of the houses were dark. He wondered if there were any people who had refused to leave their homes. Where was Miss Eells? Anthony felt she ought to be there by now. It looked as though most of the people from his part of town had already arrived. The parking lot was jammed. Darn it, why didn't she get here? Anthony wanted to talk to her about the great discovery he had made.

And then a horrible thought struck him.

What if Miss Eells had had an accident? What if she were lying unconscious somewhere? There was no one around to help if something had happened. She might lie there for hours and then drown when the flood waters came rushing into the town.

Anthony didn't know why this worrisome thought had come into his head, but once it was there, he couldn't seem to get it out. The trouble was, it all seemed so very likely that Miss Eells *would* have an accident of some kind.

Anthony began to get panicky. The more he thought, the more thoroughly convinced he became that something had happened to her. He looked around. He felt helpless. What could he do? At the end of the driveway was a police car. Its blue light revolved slowly, and its motor was idling. Maybe he'd better try to get help.

He ran down the drive to the police car and rapped on the window. The policeman rolled down the window.

"Yeah? Whaddaya want?"

"Please, officer, there's a friend of mine down in the town and—and I think maybe something happened to her. Could—could I maybe go down to her house with you and make sure she's okay?"

The policeman was tired. It had been a long, hard night, and he didn't feel like being polite. "Look, kid, if I ran around to every place that everybody asked me to go, I wouldn't know which end was up. Your friend is okay. What'd you say his name was?"

"It's not a man, it's a lady. It's Miss Eells, the lady that runs the library."

"Oh, her. Well, don't you worry about her, son. She's a pretty smart old chicken. She's probably already up here in one of these rooms, takin' a snooze."

"Yeah, but she promised to meet me . . ."

At this point the policeman's car radio started to squawk. A red light on the panel lit up. "Sorry, kid, I got work to do," said the cop. He rolled up the window and started fiddling with the dial on his car radio. Then he picked up the microphone, said something into it, and drove off.

Anthony stood there in the middle of the driveway, watching him go. Should he go find another cop? No, it wouldn't do any good. Everybody would think he was just a crazy kid with a lot of silly ideas. He stood there thinking a moment longer. Then he set out on a dead run down the driveway. He was running fast, pumping his arms. He passed the stone gateposts at the entrance

131

to the academy's grounds, then slogged downhill through the wet, elbows and knees pumping up and down like pistons. It would be a long run, but he could do it. He was a wiry kid, and a good runner. He would save Miss Eells if he could.

Anthony ran through the deserted streets. He splashed in and out of puddles. The gutters were running with rainwater. He could hear it gurgling down into the storm sewers as he ran. *I'll save you, Miss Eells*, he said to himself as he ran. *Don't worry, I'll save you.*

Another thought was running through his mind, too. It was about the treasure. He knew where it was now, or he thought he knew. It was in the library. Miss Eells had said that the treasure would be safe there for the time being, but Anthony wasn't so sure about that. He was still worried that someone might sneak in and grab it before he got there.

Anthony was running down Division Street now. The houses were all dark. Nobody was around, not a soul. The evacuation of the lower part of town had been pretty complete. Once, as Anthony was crossing a street, he saw a jeep cruising past several blocks away. It was probably somebody sent by his mother, he thought, somebody who wanted to drag him back to the academy. Well, he wasn't going. Not till he had found Miss Eells. His mother thought he was stupid, but grown-ups were the ones who were stupid, not him. Maybe he had been wrong about the treasure, but he was on the right trail now. As soon as he had made sure that Miss Eells was safe and sound, they would go get the treasure together, and then wouldn't everybody be surprised! Including Hugo Philpotts. Anthony grinned. It was a determined, stubborn grin. He would fix them, he would show them all. His legs ached, and there was a pain in his side, but he gritted his teeth and ran on.

Sometime later, Anthony turned onto the sidewalk in front of Miss Eells's house. It had stopped raining, but lightning still flashed now and then. Thunder rumbled in the distance. The storm was moving off across the bluffs, into Wisconsin. Anthony looked like a drowned rat. He was dripping with rain and sweat. Halfway down Division Street, he had torn off his raincoat and hat so that he could run faster. He saw a light burning in Miss Eells's living room. Her garage doors were closed, so he really couldn't tell if her car was there or not. When he caught his breath, he ran up the sidewalk and banged on the front door. He pushed the bell several times. Without waiting for an answer, he turned the doorknob. The door swung open.

Inside it was empty. Miss Eells was not to be found. Anthony turned and walked back toward the front door.

"Help! Help!" A cry, faint and feeble, came from the cellar.

Anthony ran back to the cellar door and looked down into the darkness. He could just barely see something or somebody lying huddled at the bottom.

"Down here . . . down here . . . please help me, I'm hurt!"

Frantically, Anthony fumbled for the switch that turned on the cellar light. He flipped it, but nothing happened. But by now his eyes were getting used to the darkness. With the hall light on, he could pick his way down. Slowly, cautiously, he started down the steps. At the bottom, he found Miss Eells.

"An—Anthony? Is that you?"

Anthony's eyes filled with tears. "Yeah, it's me, Miss Eells," he said in a thick, choked voice. "Are you all right?"

Miss Eells made a funny sound that might have been

a laugh. "Not really," she said faintly. "I seem to—to keep passing out. And I've—cut myself some—somehow. That's two bumps on the head in one year. Not good. Not good." Miss Eells's voice was wandering and dreamy, as if she were talking in her sleep. She tried to raise herself on her hands, but the effort was too much. She collapsed, unconscious, on the cellar floor.

Chapter 14

Anthony didn't know what to do. He figured Miss Eells must have fallen down the steps, and he had always been told that it was dangerous to move somebody who had had a bad fall. After all, they might have some broken bones. But if he left Miss Eells down there and the flood waters got into the town, then she would drown. He stood there trying to make up his mind. Could he drag her up those stairs? He was just a kid, but on the other hand, she was a small woman. She probably didn't weigh very much. He knelt down by her side. He put his hands on her shoulders and was just about to turn her onto her back when she came to.

"Anthony?"

"Yeah, Miss Eells? What is it?"

"I—I think I could make it up the stairs if you would —help me."

Anthony felt a lump in his throat. He saw the puddle of blood on the cellar floor, and when Miss Eells raised her head, he saw the ragged gash on her scalp and her hair matted with dried blood. He almost felt as if he were going to be sick, but he fought the feeling down. "Okay, Miss Eells. Let's give it a try."

Slowly, with Anthony's help, she raised herself to her knees. Then Anthony put his arm around her waist and made her put her arm around his neck. He rose, and she rose with him, shudderingly and slowly. When Miss Eells took her first step, she almost fell down, but she stopped herself, and after a slight pause, she began to shuffle forward. Up the steps they went, one step at a time. It seemed to take forever, but at last they made it to the top.

Still hanging onto Anthony, Miss Eells hobbled into the kitchen and sat down. Now she began to give directions. She told Anthony to tear up a clean dishtowel so she could use it to bandage her head. Anthony got a pair of shears out of the drawer next to the sink and did as he was told. When the bandage was in place, Miss Eells asked for a glass of water. Anthony got it for her. She drank it all down in one swallow.

"Aah! That feels better! *Much* better!"

Anthony sat down on a chair nearby and eyed Miss Eells anxiously.

"Miss Eells, doncha think we better get the heck out of here? There might be a flood any minute!"

Miss Eells stared vaguely into her empty water glass. It was hard to tell if she was punchy or just very relaxed. She had seemed clear-headed enough while she was giving Anthony directions about the bandage, but now

137

she seemed to be falling back into a kind of stupor, a state where nothing much mattered to her at all. "Hmmm . . . yes, I suppose that would be wise," said Miss Eells carelessly. Then she looked up suddenly and blinked her eyes. "Good grief, do you suppose we really *will* be flooded?"

"I dunno, Miss Eells, but I think we better get you over to the hospital."

Miss Eells said nothing. Anthony was beginning to feel desperate. What was he going to do with her? For the time being, all thoughts of Alpheus Winterborn's treasure had vanished from his mind. Miss Eells was hurt, and he had to help her. He had to get her to the hospital. Or better yet, call an ambulance. Sure. That would be the thing to do.

"Miss Eells?"

"Yes, Anthony?"

"I think we better get you to the hospital. Where's your phone?"

Miss Eells looked confused. "Phone? Oh . . . well, it's out in the front hall. By the way, could I have another glass of water?"

Anthony hurriedly poured Miss Eells another glass of water. Then he went out into the hall and hunted for the phone. There it was, on a dusty little table next to the coat tree. He picked up the receiver and put it to his ear. Nothing. Not even a rattle. He jiggled the little buttons on the receiver rest. Still nothing. The phone was dead.

Anthony slammed the phone down and went back to the kitchen. Miss Eells was still sitting there with the water glass in her hand.

"Miss Eells, the phone is dead. I don't know what to do. Do—do you think you could walk to the hospital?"

"I guess so," she said uncertainly. "How far is it?"

This was a further sign to Anthony that Miss Eells was pretty far gone. She knew the town like the back of her hand, and when she started asking things like "How far is the hospital?" it was a sure sign that she wasn't very with it.

Anthony helped Miss Eells to her feet, and they started off. Out into the hall, down the front steps, down the walk. Miss Eells hobbled along at Anthony's side, as helpless as a small child. Without his arm to cling to, she would have collapsed.

They had gone about half a block in the direction of the hospital when Miss Eells passed out. Anthony suddenly felt a heavy weight sagging against his arm, and Miss Eells fell to her knees, dragging him down with her. Anthony managed somehow to get her laid out on the sidewalk; then he started slapping her cheeks. "Wake up, Miss Eells! Wake up! We've still got a long way to go! Come on, wake up!" After a few minutes, she came to and staggered to her feet. Leaning heavily on Anthony, she started off again. Half a block more, and she passed out again.

It was useless, and Anthony knew it. They'd never get to the hospital at this rate. But where could they go? The library! Of course! Why hadn't he thought of it before! It was on high ground, and there might be a phone in working order there. Vague visions of the treasure flitted before Anthony's eyes again, but he ignored them. The important thing now was to save Miss Eells. Carefully he steered her across the street. They were headed toward Levee Park now, and the library.

Miss Eells hobbled across the park with Anthony holding her up. The walks were lined with benches, and every now and then Miss Eells would have to sit down on one and rest. She kept getting dizzy, and Anthony was afraid she might pass out again. Somehow, though, she managed to recover from each of these new attacks of dizziness. Each time she got up and moved on.

They were about halfway across the park when the street lights went out. The power station was down by the river, and somebody had decided to shut down the dynamos for fear that the river water would get in and short them out. The library loomed ahead of them, a dark shadow against a dark sky. They were approaching the library from the rear, and the tall shadow of the tower appeared on the right. Anthony gasped. He looked, and he blinked, and he looked again. There was a light on. A light in the tower.

"My gosh!" Anthony exclaimed. "Lookit!"

Miss Eells raised her head. She laughed an odd, silly little laugh. "Now that's funny, isn't it? A light in the tower room! But there isn't any light up there, is there?" Miss Eells shook her head and stared strangely at Anthony. "Anthony," she said suddenly, "why are we going to the library?"

"Because of the flood," said Anthony.

Miss Eells looked vague again. "Oh. Oh, yes. I do seem to remember. But you know, there really isn't any electric light up in the tower. No fixture of any kind. I'm quite sure of that. Every time I go up there, I have to take a flashlight with me."

Anthony looked up at the tower again. Sure enough, there was a light on in the tower room. Suddenly, Anthony had a creepy feeling. Maybe the ghost of Alpheus Winterborn had come back. What if he was waiting for them at the top of the tower stairs? Anthony shook off this feeling. Ghosts were the least of his worries right now.

Following a narrow cement walk, Miss Eells and Anthony made their way around to the front of the library. The storm clouds were gone now. The sky was clear, and the moon was out. Under its light, the library cast a shadow, a vast, irregular, dark pall that fell across the sidewalk. Just as they rounded the northwest corner of the library, where the tower was, Miss Eells and Anthony stepped out of the shadow. Anthony felt as if they were stepping out into sunlight. The shadow of Alpheus Winterborn's old stone castle chilled him to the bone.

When they reached the front steps of the library, Anthony stopped for a second. Miss Eells, who was being led along by him, stopped, too. Anthony turned and peered out across the park toward the riverbank. He could just barely see the wall of sandbags and the river glimmering beyond it. He wondered how high the river was now and whether any of the water was seeping through into the park. Then he saw something move. There were men down there, keeping watch on the river.

Anthony hesitated. He started to call to the men. Perhaps they could help Miss Eells; she certainly wasn't in very good shape. Her cut had stopped bleeding, but she was acting funny, and Anthony knew she ought to see a doctor. He glanced at her again. She stood there at his side, staring blearily out toward the river, but her eyes didn't seem to be seeing much. *I'd better get her inside first*, Anthony told himself.

As they climbed the library steps, Anthony fumbled in his pocket for the key to the front door. He always carried it with him, and he smiled as his hand closed over the small, cold piece of metal. But when he pulled the key out and started to stick it in the lock, he got a big surprise. The door was already open. One of the two big panes of glass in the door had been shattered. The bolt had been turned from the inside, and the door stood slightly ajar.

Now Anthony was frightened. Somebody *was* inside the library. He felt his heart pounding. He wanted to take Miss Eells and run. But then he told himself that he was being cowardly and foolish. The pane of glass might have been shattered by some kid with a stone. The light in the tower might have been a reflection from the lights down by the river, or the moon. Miss Eells might have forgotten to lock the door when she closed up the library, and the wind might have blown the door open. Anthony knew he was kidding himself, but he wanted to believe the little explanations he was making up in his mind. He was scared of what he might run into when he walked inside. But he had to get to a phone.

He took a deep breath, steeled himself, and stepped forward. He grabbed the knob and flung the door wide open. "Come on, Miss Eells," he said, giving her his arm.

Miss Eells thanked Anthony in a mumbly voice and tottered on into the dark front hall of the library. Up the inside steps they went, and through a set of swinging doors. The Hoosac Public Library was a strange place in the darkness. Gaping black arches opened on either side, and at the rear of the building shadowy rows of books dreamed in the moonlight. Moving carefully, Anthony picked his way along till he came to an upholstered bench that was built into one wall. Gently, he eased Miss Eells down onto the seat.

"You lie down and try to get some rest, Miss Eells," Anthony whispered. "I'm gonna see if the phone is working."

"Very well." Miss Eells sighed. She leaned her head

142

back against the corner of the bench and fell asleep immediately in that position.

Meanwhile, Anthony was over at the circulation desk groping for the phone. Finally he located it and lifted the receiver. Dead—just like the other one.

As he put the phone down, he felt deep despair. From the bench came the sound of Miss Eells's steady, soft snoring. "Oh, my gosh!" he said out loud. "*Now* what am I gonna do?"

Here was Miss Eells, asleep, helpless, maybe dying. He was a pretty strong kid for his age, but he couldn't carry her from there to the hospital. Even if he managed to wake her up again, the flood might catch them if they tried to go on foot. Then he thought about the light he had seen in the tower room. He dismissed the idea of ghosts—that seemed ridiculous—but then who or what *was* up there? Maybe someone had taken refuge in the tower because of the flood. Miss Pratt, maybe, from the branch library! Did she know about the tower room? Whoever it was up there, Anthony felt that he ought to go find out. He needed company—and help—badly.

Anthony fumbled around among the shelves under the desk—he remembered that he had seen a flashlight there once. Ah. There it was. He tried it, and it worked. He got up and started down the stairs that led to the cellar. He had some qualms about what he was doing, but he fought them down.

With the aid of the flashlight, he found the stairs to the tower room. Up the steps he crept. Once or twice he stopped, but each time he pulled himself together and went on. He was almost at the top of the stairs when he saw that the door of the tower room was ajar. Light streamed out from inside the room. Quietly, steadily, he climbed the last two stairs. When he got to the door, he just stopped and stared.

There was a trap door in the ceiling of the tower room—Anthony had noticed it before. It hung open, and a rope ladder hung down from it. A man was standing beside it, staring up at the black opening. The man was Hugo Philpotts.

Chapter 15

HUGO PHILPOTTS was really quite a sight. He was wearing a red and black cotton shirt, dungarees, tennis shoes, and a big floppy cap with a peak on it. Around his waist was a wide leather belt, the kind that window-washers use. There were wide flaps hanging off the front of the belt, and there were metal clips on the ends of the flaps. In one hand Mr. Philpotts held a hammer and a hacksaw. In the other, he carried a chrome-plated portable searchlight with a swinging handle and a basket-shaped rest on the bottom.

Anthony almost laughed. Mr. Philpotts was one of those very stuffy people who would make you imagine that they slept in a suit and tie at night. And now to see him in this get-up!

Hugo Philpotts turned suddenly. He shone the beam of the searchlight at Anthony. "Well, well. So it's you! I might have known. I saw a couple of people come out of the shadows at the corner of the library, but I couldn't make out who they were. Who's the other one? Is that old hag with you?"

"If you mean Miss Eells, yeah, she's downstairs. And she's hurt bad. She fell down her cellar stairs and cut her head open. Mr. Philpotts, please will you help me carry her to the hospital? She might die if we don't do something fast!"

Hugo stared stonily at Anthony. "More lies, eh? You're full of them, boy, aren't you? I know why you two are here. You're after the treasure, aren't you?"

Anthony just gaped at him.

Hugo laughed harshly. "Surprised, eh? So was I when I got home this evening and picked up my phone to find myself listening to you explaining to your dear friend Miss Eells how you had figured out where the treasure was. Crossed wires because of the storm, I suppose. Or perhaps it was the ghost of my dear Uncle Alpheus who arranged your call to be on my phone. Ha, ha. In any case, as I was saying, I was surprised. And I have to hand it to you. You are a very clever boy. So the reindeer weather vane conceals my treasure, does it?"

Suddenly Hugo Philpotts stopped talking. A wonderful idea had just occurred to him.

For some time now, he had been standing in the tower room, brooding. He was brooding because he couldn't get up the courage to go out on the roof, climb up the ladder, and get the treasure out of the weather vane. Finding the entrance to the tower room had been easy enough. Hugo had worked in the library when he was a young man, home on vacation from Harvard, so he knew the secret of the hidden door. And he had come prepared to do a little surgery on the bronze reindeer. The safety belt he wore was a window-washer's belt that he had taken from a storeroom at the bank. He had a hammer and a hacksaw and a screwdriver for prying. And the time was perfect. With everybody—well, practically everybody—gone from the lower end of town, there was not much likelihood that anyone would see him. But when he stuck his head out of the trap-door opening and looked up at the spindly iron ladder that led to the weather vane, he nearly had heart failure. The ladder was old and rickety and rusty. One or two of the rungs were missing, and when he seized the ladder in both hands and shook it, the ladder went up and down with a loud clattering and squeaking noise. Several of the bolts that held the ladder to the shingled roof were loose. It didn't look like a very safe ladder at all. In fact, as Hugo Philpotts said to himself with a shudder, anyone who tried to climb that ladder might very well end up dead.

Hugo stood looking at Anthony. He rubbed his chin and smiled unpleasantly. "Young man," he said slowly, "how would you like to earn a little, uh, leniency for your father?"

Anthony gave Hugo a blank stare. "I—I dunno what you mean, Mr. Philpotts."

Hugo came closer to Anthony. He put his hand on Anthony's shoulder and smiled in his usual cold, creepy way. "I mean just this. If you'll climb up the ladder and get the treasure out for me, I promise you that I will not deal harshly with your father. Once I have the treasure, I will deal with your father—generously."

At first Anthony was dumbfounded. Why did Hugo Philpotts want Anthony to go up the ladder instead of him? But then it came to him—Hugo was afraid. Anthony hadn't seen the ladder, so he didn't know that Hugo had good reason to be afraid. Anthony grinned smugly. He wasn't scared of heights, and he was a good climber. It was strange to think that this big, pompous man was scared to do something that any kid could do.

Still, Anthony didn't like the idea very much. He was worried about Miss Eells, and he didn't see why he should do Hugo Philpotts's dirty work for him. "Mr. Philpotts," he said, "before I go do any climbing, I want you to write out a promise for me."

Hugo's eyebrows rose. "A promise? What kind of promise?"

"I want you to write down that you'll let my dad keep his store. And that you'll help me get Miss Eells to the hospital as soon as we get the treasure."

Hugo's eyebrows shot up again. "Oh. That's what you want, is it? Well, I'm sorry. I'm afraid you're out of luck. I still have what they call the whip hand in this little chariot race, and I'm not going to give it over to you. For all I know, there may not be anything inside that ridiculous weather vane. And then wouldn't I look foolish for making a lot of promises to *you*! No, young man. No promises. You've got to help me, whether you want to or not."

If looks could kill, the look Anthony gave Hugo Philpotts would have finished him off then and there. Anthony was boiling over with rage and bitterness. He wanted to pick up a chair and smash it over Hugo's head, the way cowboys did in the movies. But he was beaten, and he knew it. He had to do what this rotten, creepy, no-good man wanted him to do. His father's life and Miss Eells's might depend on it. He would get it over with in a hurry.

"Okay, Mr. Philpotts," said Anthony in a low voice. "I'll do what you say."

As Anthony got ready to make the climb, Hugo unbuckled the window-washer's belt and offered it to him. He explained that the spring clips on the ends of the two hanging flaps were supposed to hook into metal rings in the window frames of the windows at the bank. But he showed Anthony how he could hook the clips together around the post of the weather vane to give himself a good solid mooring while he hacked, sawed, or pounded at the reindeer. This seemed like a good idea to Anthony, but, when he tried the belt on, it was too large and wouldn't buckle. The belt had been made for a full-grown man.

"Ah, but a hole can be made," said Hugo in his smug, superior way. He got a hammer and a nail out of the tool box he had brought with him, and with the belt laid out flat on the floor, he put the point of the nail on the belt's tongue and tapped with his hammer. When he was through, there was a new hole in the belt. Now Anthony could wear it.

Anthony felt strange as he buckled the big, heavy leather belt around himself. The flaps hanging off the front seemed awkward and silly, and it occurred to him that they would get in his way when he was climbing. But when he had tucked the flaps into the front of the belt, he felt better. He figured he could manage that way. There were some loops in the belt, meant to hold pieces of window-washing equipment; Anthony stuck the hammer into one of them. From a dangling metal clip he hung the small hacksaw that Hugo had brought with him. There was a screwdriver, too, for prying, but Anthony decided to leave it behind. He felt overloaded even as he was.

149

"Okay," said Anthony in a thick voice. "I guess I'm ready."

"After you, young man," Hugo said, stepping aside.

Anthony started up. The rope ladder swung and swayed, but it held firm. When he got to the top, he clambered out into the small, dusty floor of the crawl space. Above him, in the darkness, he saw a square patch of deep midnight blue and some stars. The trap door that led out onto the roof lay open.

"Go on out! The door's open!" called Hugo from below. "The ladder starts just above the opening. I'll be right behind you."

Thanks a bunch, thought Anthony, but he said nothing. He bit his lip grimly, took a deep breath, and stuck his head out of the hole.

Suddenly a wave of dizziness and fear swept over him. The trees and the river and the walks below him blurred and shimmered, got closer and then farther away, and then closer again, as if he were looking at them through a telescope that was going in and out of focus all the time. Anthony had never had an attack like this before. Maybe it was because he was tired. Cold sweat ran down his face, and he could feel a knot forming in his stomach. He closed his eyes and heard the blood roaring in his ears.

"What's the matter? Why didn't you go on up?" Hugo called up to him from below. "Get a move on. We can't stay here all night, you know."

"O-okay," Anthony stammered. He felt another wave of chilly sickness pass over him. Then his head cleared. "I'm okay now," he said.

"Then go on out. Stop stalling."

"I'm not stalling, I just felt—kinda sick, that's all."

"You'll feel better when you get outside. Go on."

Anthony stuck his head out of the little square opening again. He turned around quickly to avoid looking down. Above him rose the sloping tower roof. It seemed as steep and as tall as the side of a mountain. The shingles glimmered gray in the moonlight. Up at the top, perched on the point of the conical roof, was the weather vane with the reindeer on it. The right front paw was raised. *That must be the way in,* thought Anthony. *Right through that raised-up leg. "Mind the prancing and pawing of each little hoof."* That was the only hoof that was prancing and pawing. Maybe the leg unscrewed or something like that. Or maybe he would have to use the hacksaw. Oh, well, he would find out, one way or another. He felt very depressed as he looked up at the reindeer. He had worked so hard to get at Alpheus Winterborn's treasure. He had sweated and slaved and worried and fretted. He had even broken his arm. Now he was climbing the ladder to get it—for somebody else. And not for just anybody, either. He was going to get it for the person he hated most in all the world.

Anthony sighed and shook his head. He gritted his teeth and put his hands on the rung above him. But as soon as he swung his foot up and started to put his weight on the ladder, something happened. The ladder groaned and shrieked. It jolted forward as if it were going to come loose. Terrified, Anthony jumped back down into the trap-door opening.

Hugo Philpotts was hanging on the rope ladder just below the opening in the ceiling of the tower room. He shone the searchlight up at Anthony. "Well, what are you waiting for? For heaven's sake, stop dilly-dallying! It'll be dawn before you know it if you keep up this way!"

"The ladder's broken," said Anthony. "It'll come off if I try to go up it."

"Nonsense," snapped Hugo. "It's—well, it's just a

little loose, that's all. But it's perfectly safe. I climbed up it myself to the top just to see." This was a lie, of course. Hugo Philpotts hadn't gone any farther up the ladder than Anthony had. To ease his conscience (what conscience he had), Hugo told himself that the boy's lighter body would make all the difference. He would be able to climb to the top once he got moving.

Anthony looked down at Hugo. Then he looked up at the ladder. He swallowed hard. He thought about Miss Eells, and his father. He would just have to try to do it. Once more, he put his hands on the rung above him and swung himself up. The ladder shrieked and shuddered as before, but it held firm. His whole weight was on it now. Slowly he started up. At each step he could feel the ladder tremble, but it stayed in place. Up one hand, then up one foot, that was how it was done. Slow but sure, one step at a time. He climbed on, and the reindeer got closer and closer. *Easy does it now*, he said to himself, *easy does it* . . .

When he was about two-thirds of the way up, Anthony saw something that made him even more frightened than he had been before. All along, he had noticed how rusty the ladder was. It was covered with a reddish-brown crust, and he could feel pieces flaking off under his hands as he gripped the rungs. But now he had reached a point where the ladder had rusted so much that it was almost in two pieces. The parallel iron bars that ran up the sides and held the rungs in place were just pitted shells at this point. He reached out and grasped one of the bars and felt it crumble and crunch under his hand. It was about as solid and reliable as a piece of macaroni. Anthony felt another wave of fear sweep over him. For a second, he was afraid that he was going to throw up. Sweat was pouring down his face, and he had to work

152

very, very hard to keep staring straight ahead of him. He had an idea of what would happen if he glanced down.

On Anthony climbed. Now he was past the rusted-out place. The top part of the ladder seemed more solidly anchored. The bolts that held it to the roof didn't slide in and out as he climbed. The bars and the rungs seemed more solid, too. Well, here he was up at the top of the roof. He could reach out and put his hand on the big post that held the weather vane in place. And there was the reindeer, its upraised hoof hovering over Anthony's head. As Anthony watched, a gust of wind hit the reindeer. It shuddered, but it didn't move. Below the reindeer were four iron bars that stuck out from the post. On the end of each bar was an iron letter. There were four of them, for the four points of the compass: N, E, S, W. When the weather vane was in working order—if it ever had been—the reindeer would have twirled around with the gusts of wind, and the upraised paw would have pointed in the direction that the wind was blowing from. But the reindeer was stuck—stuck, Anthony guessed, because it was off balance. And it was off balance because there was something inside it. If it was the treasure, he wondered how old Winterborn managed to put it in there.

Anthony sighed and looked up. His hands were on the topmost rung of the ladder, but he really wasn't high enough up to work on the reindeer. Then he had an idea. He could use the bars with the letters on them for hand-holds. Cautiously, he reached up. His fingers closed around the bar with "E" on its end. When he had a firm grip on the bar, he pulled his body higher. Now he was up under the reindeer. He could bump his head on its underbelly. The bars were chest-high on him now. With his feet on the rung below and one hand on the bar, he reached down and slid the flaps, one by one, out of the front of the belt. But he needed both hands to lead the flaps around behind the post. For an instant or two he would have to balance on his feet.

Anthony stared rigidly ahead. He tried hard not to think of where he was. For an awful second, he teetered on tiptoe, with his chest braced against the iron bar. With trembling hands he led the flaps around behind the iron post and tried to hook them together. He fumbled and bumped the clasps together for what seemed like ages. Then he felt himself losing his balance, so he dropped the flaps and clung to the post for dear life. He closed his eyes and shuddered, and then he began to get the awful feeling that the tower was swaying under him. Finally, the sick, dizzy, swaying feeling began to go away, and he opened his eyes. With a mighty effort of the will, he kept himself from looking down. Once more, he let go of the post, slowly, one hand at a time. Balancing on tiptoe again, he led the flaps once more around behind the post and tried to make them snap together. Click-click. He had done it.

Clinging to the post, Anthony cried from sheer relief. Then, when he had calmed down a bit, he looked up.

In the moonlight, he could see the reindeer quite clearly. He saw the curls of bronze hair on its body, and the cloven hoof of the upraised front paw. The reindeer's sides were spotted and streaked with pigeon droppings, and the whole figure was covered with that greenish kind of rust that forms on bronze or copper objects when they have been out in the weather for years and years.

Anthony looked closely at the upraised leg. He wanted to see if there was some joint or crack at the place where the leg met the body. There was. Good. But when he reached up and tried to jiggle the leg, he got nowhere.

155

It wouldn't budge. Did it unscrew, like the lid on a mayonnaise jar? Anthony gripped the hoof firmly and tried to twist. No dice. It wouldn't move. Sighing, he reached down and started to unbuckle the hacksaw from his belt. It dangled at his side, like a sword. It took a good deal of fiddling to undo the clasp with one hand, but he managed. Now he had the hacksaw in his hand. Getting as firm a grip as he could on the crossbar with his left hand, he reached up with his right hand and started to saw.

But Anthony's hands were slippery with sweat, and he was attacking the reindeer at a bad angle, from underneath. And he was using the arm he had broken to wield the hacksaw; it hadn't set quite right, and it didn't always behave properly. Anthony hadn't made more than two or three swipes with the saw when it slipped from his grasp. It sailed up over the leg and fell onto the slates of the roof. Anthony heard it slide down, clatter, clatter, clatter, all the way to the bottom.

Anthony felt helpless. Totally and utterly helpless. He had failed. Hugo Philpotts would get mad now, and who knew what he would do?

But then Anthony remembered that he still had the hammer with him. He might be able to bang on the leg till it dropped off and get the treasure out that way. With one hand still clenched firmly on the bar, he reached down and eased the hammer up out of the loop on his belt. He shifted the heavy implement around in his hand until he had a good tight grip on it. And then he started to pound at the leg.

Blong! Blong!

Anthony's mouth dropped open, and he stopped pounding. He was startled by the sound he had made. Since the deer was made of bronze, it rang like an alarm bell when it was hit.

An alarm bell! People would hear it for miles around!

Anthony grinned. A wonderful idea had occurred to him. He was sick of playing errand boy for Hugo Philpotts. What if he did get mad? It wouldn't matter— Anthony knew what he had to do.

He hauled off and struck the leg of the deer again. And again and again and again. *Blong! Blong! Blong! Blong!*

"Stop it! Stop it! What are you doing, you little fool? Stop!" It was Hugo Philpotts calling. He was standing at the bottom of the ladder and staring up in astonishment and horror.

Anthony paid no attention. He went on pounding. The reindeer rattled and rang, sending its loud, high-pitched bell-sound out across the night.

Chapter 16

ALTHOUGH his arm was getting tired, Anthony kept on pounding. He was flailing away with a maniacal fury now, and the blows of the hammer were hitting all over the reindeer, not just on the leg. He banged on the deer's bronze underbelly, on its sides, and even on its neck. When he hit the reindeer's belly, the sound was very loud and bell-like. Over and over the hammer rose and fell.

"You fool! You fool! Stop, for God's sake!" Hugo Philpotts had climbed halfway up the ladder. He was bellowing at Anthony with one hand cupped to his mouth. But it was no use. With the noise he was making, Anthony could hardly have heard him even if he had wanted to. But now, over the clanging and banging rose a louder noise. A siren. Fire trucks were coming.

Anthony stopped pounding and started to cheer. "It worked!" he yelled. "My alarm bell worked!" People were coming. They would save Miss Eells. They would discover Hugo Philpotts. Everything would be all right.

A small crowd was beginning to gather on the lawn below. Anthony didn't know it, but the flood crisis was over. People were beginning to pour back into town. The men who had been manning the sandbag wall had heard the bell and had figured the library was on fire. So had the firemen in the firehouse on Eddy Street. They hadn't stopped to consider whether or not there was a bell in the library tower. They had simply piled into their trucks, and now they were on their way. In fact, they were almost there.

Anthony went on bashing the reindeer with his hammer. Hugo Philpotts was hanging below on the ladder, trying to decide what to do. But then—quite suddenly —the decision was made for him. With a terrific groaning and shrieking of metal, the part of the ladder he was hanging on began to pull loose from the roof. Bolts popped and snapped. The ladder broke in two at the very rusty point that Anthony had noticed, and the section that Hugo was clinging to leaned lazily over sideways. It groaned and creaked and bent, and for a horrible instant, Hugo thought that it would break off entirely and throw him to the ground four stories below. But it didn't. It just stopped in its bent-over position. And there he was, hanging between earth and sky— Hugo Philpotts, first vice-president of the First National Bank of Hoosac, in sneakers and jeans, in the middle of the night, with people staring at him from below! Down on the ground, with a roaring of motors and a piercing wail of sirens, fire trucks were pulling up on the gravel drive in front of the library.

Meanwhile, at the top of the tower, Anthony swayed

on his dizzy perch. His section of the ladder—the top part—had held firm. The rung he had been standing on was still under his feet, and the safety belt was still hooked around the stout post that the weather vane was mounted on.

"Help! Help! For God's sake, somebody help me!"

Anthony heard the yelling and looked down. He saw the bent-over section of the ladder hanging out in space, with Hugo Philpotts clinging to it for dear life. The shock of this incredible sight made Anthony hold on tighter to the weather vane. Then he looked back up at the reindeer. Its leg and underbelly were scarred where the hammer had hit. There were bright golden scratches on the corroded green surface. And now Anthony noticed something that he hadn't noticed before: On the up-raised leg of the reindeer, up near the place where the leg joined the body, was a button. It had been cleverly made to look like a little curl of hair, but it was a button, like the button on a doorbell. With his wild, aimless bashing, Anthony had knocked some of the green crud off the area around it, and now it lay exposed quite clearly.

Anthony hefted the hammer in his hand. He got a firm grip, raised the hammer, and struck the button a single sharp blow. *Sproing!* A powerful spring inside the reindeer uncoiled, and the leg, moving on a concealed hinge, swung open like a door. When this happened, something else happened, too—a package slid out of the hole in the reindeer's body. It slid right out into Anthony's arms.

With a startled gasp, Anthony dropped the hammer and grabbed the package. With his free hand, he clutched it tightly to his side. The package was about the size of a small loaf of bread, and it was wrapped in

161

gray cloth and tied up in cord. A gust of wind hit Anthony, and he teetered on his perch. It was hard to hang on with one hand, but he managed it, and the safety belt helped. A wave of dizziness passed over him again. He was scared to death, but he also felt very happy. He was sure that this was the treasure, here, clasped to his side. All he had to do now was hang on till somebody rescued him.

From below came the shouts of firemen. Men were giving orders, pulling out hoses, cranking up ladders. One truck had a huge spotlight on it, and the spotlight was rotated till it shone over Hugo Philpotts and Anthony. Now the long ladder on the hook-and-ladder truck swung around on its swivel. It rose up, and with a loud clattering and clicking of gears, it started to make itself longer. Up the long ladder rose, up, up, up the side of the tall stone tower. Now the tip of the ladder had reached the base of the tower roof, and it was up even with Hugo. Its tip tapped the shingles near him. A fireman in a shiny black helmet started to climb. It didn't take him long to reach Hugo. Carefully, gently, the fireman helped the frightened man climb down off the swaying, rusty ladder and onto the fire truck's ladder. Then down they went, the fireman and Hugo, slowly, one rung at a time.

A couple of newsmen with flash cameras had arrived on the scene in a car. Flash bulbs popped. A loud, raucous cheer went up from the crowd. Many of them recognized Hugo.

"Who is it, anyway?" somebody yelled.

"Hey, it's Philpotts, the guy down at the bank!"

"What the heck was he doing up there?"

"I dunno. Checkin' up on the weather, maybe. Yay, Hugo! Let's give him three cheers."

Everybody yelled and laughed and hooted. Three more loud, raucous cheers went up. Hugo Philpotts, stony-faced and shivering, was helped down off the truck. He stood on the ground with a blanket over his shoulders.

Up above, Anthony still hung on. His left hand, the hand on the bar, was getting numb, but he stubbornly clung to his prize with his other hand. He would rather have died than let it go. Grimly, he stared straight ahead at the post of the weather vane. He didn't dare look down again.

Now the ladder was rising higher. Click, grind, rattle-rattle! Now it was just under his feet. The fireman was climbing again. When he got to the top, the fireman started talking gently to Anthony. He told him to throw down whatever he was holding and take his hand. But Anthony wouldn't drop the parcel. Finally, the fireman persuaded him to let him put it in the pocket of his coat—the fireman's big shiny rubber coat had a deep pocket in the side of it, and the package slid in easily. Next, the fireman told Anthony to undo the clasps on the safety belt. With both hands free, this wasn't such a difficult job. After a little fumbling, Anthony got the snaps unsnapped. All the while he was working at the snaps, the fireman's big strong hands were around his waist. He wasn't going to let Anthony fall.

When the safety belt was finally unhooked, the fireman, who had been talking reassuringly the whole time, eased Anthony down from his perch to the rungs of the ladder. He asked Anthony to follow him slowly down the ladder. But now that the real danger had passed, Anthony went all to pieces. He shuddered and shivered and clung rigidly to the ladder. "I don't wanna go down! I'm scared!" he wailed.

The fireman smiled sympathetically at Anthony. He

had seen cases like this before. Without hesitating, he turned and bellowed an order down to the men who were working the controls of the ladder. More rattling and grinding of gears. Slowly, the top section of the ladder began to slide down with Anthony and the fireman still on it. Click, click, one rung at a time. The ladder went on collapsing like a telescope until the two sections were lying one on top of the other. Now the ladder was only half as long as it had been before. More gear-grinding. The ladder swung around in a big arc and slowly laid itself down on top of the long red truck. A dazed Anthony found himself being led by the hand along the top of the truck and down some steps to the ground.

And there, standing next to the truck, were his mother and his father and Keith. They looked anxious and frightened and happy, too, all at the same time.

"Where's Miss Eells?" asked Anthony weakly.

But nobody seemed to hear him.

Mrs. Monday rushed forward and grabbed him in her arms and hugged him violently. "Anthony, Anthony, oh, I'm *so* glad you're safe! What happened? What happened to you? Why did you run away? Did that man over there kidnap you? What happened? Oh, I'm *so* glad you're back, *I'm so glad*!"

Anthony felt very happy. His mother hadn't seemed so glad to see him in a long, long time, he thought. Now Keith and his parents were all talking to him at once, bombarding him with questions that he couldn't answer. He felt dizzy and confused. It was almost as if he were walking around in a dream. In the midst of all this, he felt a tap on his arm. He turned around, and there was the fireman who had rescued him.

"Excuse me, young man, but I believe this belongs to you. You had it in your hand when you were up there, and you wouldn't let go of it for love or money." The fireman held out the package that had fallen out of the reindeer. Anthony grabbed it and hugged it to his chest.

"Gee, thanks, mister. Thanks an awful lot!"

Now Mrs. Monday turned to the fireman, and for a moment it looked as if she were going to hug him. "Oh, thank you, thank you so much! What is your name, officer? I'm going to see that you get a medal for this!"

The fireman smiled politely and touched the brim of his helmet. "All in the line of duty, ma'am. Glad to see the boy is safe and sound again." And with that he turned and went back to his truck. The newsmen who had taken Hugo Philpotts's picture now crowded around Anthony and snapped his picture, too.

And now someone else arrived on the scene: Miss Eells. With her head still swathed in its bloody bandage, she came tottering down the front steps of the library and rushed over to Anthony. She threw her arms around him and gave him a very large hug.

"Anthony, Anthony! My Lord, what on earth is going on around here, anyway? I remember falling down the steps in my house and hitting my head, and then I woke up here just now and heard all this racket going on outside!"

"I found the treasure, Miss Eells!" Anthony exclaimed. All his fear had melted away now, and he was feeling very proud about what he had done. "It's Alpheus Winterborn's treasure! It's really here, right here in this package!"

"If it *is* Alpheus Winterborn's treasure, it belongs to me—I mean, it belongs to the Winterborn family, and I am a member of that family." This, of course, was Hugo Philpotts talking. He had been standing next to the fire engine and shivering under his blanket, but now, seeing Anthony amid the little knot of people that had gathered around him, he had stepped forward. He stood stiffly, glowering at them all in turn, and then he shoved his way forward and stretched his hands toward the package that Anthony was holding. "It's mine, you filthy little wretch! Give it to me!" he snapped.

Mr. Monday stepped in between Anthony and Hugo. There was an angry frown on his face, and his fists were doubled up. "Who the heck are you calling a little wrench?"

"Wretch," said Hugo, correcting him.

"Well, whatever it was, you don't have any right to call my son names. What the heck were you doin' up there on that roof, anyway?"

"None of your business," sniffed Hugo. "I'll take care of you when the time comes," he added with a malicious gleam in his eye.

Mr. Monday was beginning to get really angry now. It looked as if he might haul off and paste Hugo one in the kisser. "What the heck do you mean?" Mr. Monday growled.

"You'll find out," Hugo muttered. He looked Mr. Monday over from head to foot and added, in a tone of utter disgust, "Yes, you'll find out soon enough, you disgusting, beer-guzzling clod."

"What did you call me? Say that again, you dirty low-life!" Mr. Monday squared off and raised his fists. Mrs. Monday, Keith, and Anthony crowded around him, pleading.

"C'mon, Dad, don't worry, he's just a dumb creep," said Keith. "Don't waste your time with him!"

"Don't do anything rash, Howard!" begged Mrs. Monday. "Think of your heart!"

"Please, Dad, don't hit him!" said Anthony. Secretly,

Anthony would have loved to see his dad lay Hugo Philpotts out on the pavement. Mr. Monday was an ex-Marine, and Anthony was sure he could make mincemeat out of Hugo. On the other hand, Anthony didn't want his dad to have another heart attack.

"Okay, okay, now break it up! Just break it up, the lot of you!" A policeman stepped in between Hugo and Mr. Monday. In a small town, everybody knows the policemen by name, and both Hugo and Mr. Monday knew this one. It was Officer Earl Swett, the policeman who had investigated the burglary at Miss Eells's house.

"That boy has some property of mine," said Hugo, pointing at Anthony. "I demand that he give it to me!"

Officer Swett rubbed his chin. He was a big burly guy with sleepy, hooded eyes. He talked slowly, and he never did things in a hurry. "Well, now, Mr. Philpotts, maybe he's got somethin' of yours, and maybe he doesn't. We'll have to sort this out later. By the way, would you kindly tell me what you were doin' up on that there roof?"

"Why don't you ask that boy what he was doing up there? He was up there, too, you know."

Officer Swett looked from Hugo to Anthony and back to Hugo again. He rubbed his chin thoughtfully. "We'll just have to sort all this out down at the station. I want you to come down tomorrow and answer a few questions."

Hugo glared haughtily at Officer Swett. "I beg your pardon? Are you talking to me?"

Officer Swett looked him in the eye. "Yes, sir. I believe I am."

"Do you know who I am?" said Hugo in his huffiest voice. He was trying very hard to be grand and majestic, but it's hard to be grand and majestic when you're wearing tennis shoes and dungarees and when you have just been pulled down off a library roof in the middle of the night.

Office Swett was beginning to lose his temper. With him it was always a very slow process, but when he lost it, people knew that they'd better watch out. He put his hands on his hips and stared curiously at Hugo, as if he were a bug that had just crawled out from under a rock. "Yeah, I know who you are, and I know where you were about five minutes ago. And that's exactly what I want to talk to you about."

"Do you understand the position I have in this community?" Hugo said in a threatening voice. "Do you know what I could do to you?"

"Yeah. You could cancel my Christmas Club," said Officer Swett, grinning.

Quite a little crowd had gathered around Hugo and the others, and everybody laughed loudly at this remark. Hugo's face got very red. "We'll see about this," he muttered. And then he turned and stalked away.

There was a lot to be talked about and taken care of, and it took a long time for everything to get thrashed out and settled. First of all, there was the matter of Miss Eells's head wound. It turned out that she had gotten a nasty scalp wound that took several stitches to close, and she had a mild concussion. But after a few days in the hospital, she was her usual busy, cheerful self. She talked a lot about the two knocks on the head that she had gotten in less than one year.

As for the treasure of Alpheus Winterborn, there was a great deal to be settled. Of course, nothing could be hidden now. It all had to come out, the whole incredible story of how Anthony had found the clues to the treasure, of how he had chased the treasure down one blind alley and then, almost by accident, had found the true path. As he told Miss Eells again later, he had been packing his bag on the night of the flood when all of a sudden he had realized that the motto BELIEVE ONLY HALF OF WHAT YOU READ applied to the poem. There were eight lines in the poem; the first four were just a decoy, a blind, and so was the message in the mirror. They led nowhere, or rather they led to a tin box with a four-leaf clover in it. But the last four lines of the poem were true, and once you saw this, it was all very simple. The poem even gave a clue as to how to get inside the reindeer without tearing the poor thing apart. And what was the treasure? What was inside the cloth-wrapped parcel? That, as they say, is the interesting part.

Chapter **17**

To whom it may concern:

I, Alpheus T. Winterborn, do hereby declare that whosoever removes the object that accompanies this document from its hiding place is the sole and rightful possessor, owner, and usufructuary of this said object. No other person has any claim upon it whatsoever.

Signed,

Alpheus T. Winterborn

We bear witness before Almighty God that the above statement was made and signed by the above-named person, *viz.*, Alpheus T. Winterborn, Esq., of Hoosac, Minnesota, of the County of Hoosac, in the United States of America.

Simon Searle

Simon Searle, Commissioner of Oaths
22 Wigmore St., London, W.2

Anthony Twitt

Anthony Twitt, Secretary to Mr. Searle

170

A piece of parchment containing this statement in Alpheus Winterborn's handwriting was one of the things in the cloth wrappings. It was signed by him and two witnesses, though it seems fairly likely that the witnesses hadn't had any idea of what they were signing. The whole thing had evidently been taken care of in London, where Alpheus Winterborn stopped on his way back from his first trip to the Holy Land. A big, fancy seal with a crown in the middle of it had been pressed into the paper at the bottom of the document. Bundled up with the document was a small, gilt-edged diary bound in green leather. It contained an account of how the object in the wrappings had been found. This account—like the document—was in Alpheus Winterborn's handwriting.

The object itself was a statue made of solid gold. It was not a very beautiful statue. In fact, the first time Anthony saw it (it was unwrapped down at the Hoosac Police Station, around dawn on the day after Anthony's climbing adventure), he thought it was just a shapeless lump. It looked like something that some grade-school kid had made out of molding clay. Two big hollow eyes were gouged out of one end of the statue, and the arms were just little spindly things stuck to the sides. The feet were squashy flat pads sticking out of the bottom of the statue. Each foot had two holes in it, and from this you might guess that the statue was meant to be nailed or screwed down onto something. The nose was just a little pointed nub between the eyes. And the mouth might have been made by someone working his finger back and forth, except that it would be hard to work your finger around in solid gold. The statue had ears, too—little mashed-up ears with gold earrings that clattered when you picked the statue up.

Without the green diary, Anthony and Miss Eells and the others might have puzzled over this lumpy little object for a long time. As it was, even with the diary, there were problems.

The diary explained how Alpheus Winterborn had gone out into the wilderness of Judea with only one guide and three days' supply of food and water. The wilderness of Judea is a barren, stony place, a maze of steep, rocky ravines. Nothing grows there. There is no water to drink. According to the account in the diary, one night Alpheus and his Arab guide camped in a little cave at the end of a steep, narrow gully. During the night, an earthquake struck, and when they woke up, Alpheus and his guide saw that a part of the rear wall of the cave had fallen in. They discovered that the rear wall was really artificial. It was a stone wall that had been built by somebody and then cleverly disguised to make it look like a natural rock wall. Behind the wall was—well, at first, Alpheus Winterborn wasn't sure. There were the remains of a wooden box, very old and very rotten. Hardly anything was left of it. In fact, it crumbled to dust when he touched it. There were some gold rings on the outside and what looked like a couple of warped poles that had been meant to be thrust through the rings so that bearers could carry the box from place to place. Held to one of the slabs of rotting wood by a pair of golden nails was a funny little figurine. A second one lay nearby. Suddenly it came to Alpheus; he had read his Bible, and he knew what he had found. He had found the Ark of the Covenant.

Anybody who has ever read the Bible knows what the Ark of the Covenant is. It is described at great length in the Bible, and it is talked about in a lot of the stories in the Old Testament. It was the most sacred object of the ancient Israelites. Only the priests of the tribe of Levi were allowed to touch it, and once, a man named Oza was struck dead by God for touching the Ark when he shouldn't have—at least, this is what the Bible says. According to legend, the Ark of the Covenant contained Moses's rod, Aaron's rod, two vases of manna (the food that God sent down in a rain from heaven to feed the Israelites when they were starving in the desert), and the tablets of the Law—two big stone slabs with the Ten Commandments written on them. When King Solomon built his great temple in the city of Jerusalem, the Ark was kept in the innermost room of the temple, a room called the Holy of Holies. Later, in the year 70 A.D., the temple and the city of Jerusalem were destroyed by the Romans. Some people later claimed that the Romans brought the Ark back to Rome as part of their loot. But no one really knew what happened to it. That is, no one knew until Alpheus Winterborn made his discovery.

Mr. Winterborn's diary went on to tell how he left his guide to keep watch over this treasure and went back to catch some sleep by the fire they had built near the mouth of the cave. But then a second earthquake hit, and the ceiling of the cave started to fall. Alpheus was able to save himself, but the guide was killed. Luckily, Alpheus had saved his compass, and this enabled him to hike to the monastery of Mar Saba, which stands perched on a tall cliff in the wilderness of Judea. All of Alpheus's food and water were left behind in the cave, buried under tons of rock along with the poor guide. But Alpheus had saved one thing—the small gold statue. He had no doubt that it was one of the two angels that were supposed to be perched up on top of the Ark. It was true that the angel didn't look much like the angels you see on

Christmas cards. But then, as Alpheus Winterborn pointed out in his scholarly way, the Israelites were forbidden to make statues that looked like any living creature. They had just been obeying God's commandment when they sculpted this ugly, dwarfish thing.

There was a big fight over the gold statue. First, there was the question of what it was. Archeologists from the University of Minnesota came down to look at it. Articles were written about it in the Minneapolis newspapers, in the *Chicago Tribune*, and even in the *New York Times* and the *Times* of London. Two representatives from the newly created nation of Israel showed up in Hoosac and claimed that if the object was really what Alpheus Winterborn said it was, it rightfully belonged to Israel and should be in a museum in Tel Aviv. More archeologists came and looked at the statue, read Alpheus Winterborn's diary, and shook their heads and went away. They couldn't make up their minds and say that the statue was, or was not, an angel from the Ark of the Covenant.

Meanwhile, another battle was going on. Who owned the statue? Hugo Philpotts claimed it was his—or that it certainly belonged to the Winterborn estate and not to a saloon-keeper's son. The city of Hoosac claimed that since the statue had been found in city property, it belonged to the city. Anthony, of course, claimed that the statue was his. And so a court battle took place. The Mondays were afraid of lawyers, and they really didn't have a family lawyer, but Miss Eells came up with one, her brother Emerson, who lived up in St. Cloud. He came down and argued the case for the Mondays in front of a judge in Hoosac. It was a long and messy trial, and what came out during it didn't make Hugo

Philpotts look very good. The whole business was dragged out into the open. Miss Eells told the judge how Hugo had tried to bully and threaten Anthony into giving him the treasure, how he had eavesdropped on the phone conversation between her and Anthony and had then decided to go get the treasure for himself, and finally, how he had made Anthony risk his life on an unsafe ladder. No mention was made of the stolen mirror. Miss Eells really didn't have any proof that Hugo had been the culprit, and she didn't want to weaken Anthony's case by making wild accusations. As it was, the case against Hugo was pretty strong. Everybody in town hated him by now, and when he took the witness stand to answer Miss Eells's accusations, people hissed and booed. In fact, there was such an uproar that the judge had to clear the courtroom.

The judge heard the case and read all the documents. He listened to the witnesses and the lawyers. He peered at the statue and turned it over in his hands. Finally he decided: The statue belonged to Anthony. The document wrapped up with the statue gave Anthony the sole right of possession, said the judge. It was true that the document was made in England and executed before an English Commissioner of Oaths (which is sort of like an American Notary Public), but the statement had been made by a United States citizen, and in any case it was a holograph statement—that is, it was in Alpheus Winterborn's own handwriting. That meant that the document was valid whether the two English gentlemen had signed it or not.

So Anthony got the statue. It was his own now. But he was not particularly attached to it, even though he and his statue had become famous. He had appeared on a TV show with it, and an article had been written about him in the *Reader's Digest*. It was entitled "Pie in the Sky: A Plucky Lad's Struggle for a Millionaire's Gold." Anthony got a little money out of this, but not much. As people sometimes find out, much to their sorrow, you can't eat fame. So Anthony decided to sell his statue and get rich. Under Emerson Eells's guidance, a sale was arranged. It was really an auction, with lots of museums bidding for the ugly little hunk of gold. The museum that won was the Oriental Institute at the University of Chicago. They paid Anthony $125,000 for the statue.

Anthony was disappointed. He had hoped he would get a million. But as Miss Eells pointed out to him, $125,000 was a lot of money. Anthony decided that he would take it.

Hugo Philpotts never made good on his threat to sell Mr. Monday's store out from under him. He had brought the bank a lot of bad publicity by his cruel and sneaky behavior, and finally he was forced to resign from his position there and move to another town. The new first vice-president of the First National Bank of Hoosac renewed Mr. Monday's lease. In fact, he did better than that. As a public gesture of good will, he gave Mr. Monday a ninety-nine–year lease on the building that housed Monday's Cigar Store. That was just as good as owning the building as far as Mr. Monday was concerned.

With $125,000 in the bank, a thriving business, a healthy husband, and a famous son, Mrs. Monday was happy at last—happier than she had ever been before. Anthony went on working at the library because he liked it, and he became better friends than ever with Miss Eells. He even bought her a special gift for trying to help him find the treasure, but mostly for just being such a wonderful friend. It was a foolproof, completely automatic tea-making machine from Marshall Field in Chicago. The machine had a hammered copper urn with an eagle on the top, and it could make enough tea to serve a hundred people.

One day during the following summer, Miss Eells asked Anthony's folks if it would be all right if she took Anthony on a trip. It would be a fairly long trip, about three hundred miles. She wanted to go down to Chicago so that Anthony could see the statue in its glass case, all mounted and labeled, in the museum. Mrs. Monday had gotten over some of her dislike for Miss Eells—she had liked the way Miss Eells had stuck up for Anthony during the trial—and so she consented.

It was a lovely trip. They drove down along the river to Dubuque and then took a road that angled off toward Chicago. The upper Mississippi Valley is very pretty in the summer. The tall limestone bluffs are covered with green leaves, except here and there where a yellowish crag thrusts up above the trees like a castle. The bluffs wind on and on into blue distances ahead, and people who have seen the Rhine Valley say that the upper Mississippi looks a lot like it.

When they got to Chicago, Miss Eells and Anthony stayed at a hotel in the Loop. They went to the movies and toured the Field Museum, rode on the el, and went to a concert in Grant Park. One day they took the Illinois Central electric train down to the University of Chicago and walked over to the Oriental Institute. Inside, the first thing they saw was the enormous winged and human-headed stone lion from the palace of King Sargon. It fills one whole wall of the high room that is the main exhibition hall of the museum. In the middle of the room stood a glass case on a tall wooden stand. Inside the case was an object that Anthony was familiar

177

with. When he and Miss Eells drew close to the case, they saw the card inside. It said:

GOLD STATUETTE OF UNKNOWN ORIGIN
Possibly Sumerian

Anthony's face fell when he read this inscription. "Hey, Miss Eells! What do they mean, unknown origin? Don't they really believe that it was one of the angels from the Ark of the Covenant?"

Miss Eells shrugged. "If by 'they' you mean the professors who run this museum, I don't have the foggiest notion of *what* they think. From what this card says, I would gather that they don't think there's enough evidence for them to say that it really is what Alpheus Winterborn claimed it was." They were both silent for a moment. "Of course, they may have a point," she added. "Old Alpheus may have made the whole story up."

Anthony felt very confused. "If they think it's a fake, why did they buy it?"

"Well, the statue is very old, and it really is one of a kind—that alone ought to make it valuable. Of course, someday the professors may change that card when they think they have some new evidence. One thing's for sure —they didn't buy the thing for its looks."

Anthony snorted. "Yeah, it looks like something I woulda made in the second grade. How come they made it look like that?"

"I dunno. I'm not an archeologist. However, I did do a little reading lately, and I read something that kind of interested me. The Jewish historian Josephus says that the angels on the ark didn't look like any creature above, or on, or under the earth, but that they looked like some

178

of the creatures that were standing around the throne of God when Moses went up on Mount Sinai to get the Ten Commandments. You can make what you like of that."

Anthony couldn't make much of what Miss Eells had told him. He walked around the case a few times and then said that he'd like to see some of the other stuff in the museum. As they were peering at some Assyrian reliefs, Miss Eells said rather suddenly, "Do your mom and dad still argue about money at night?"

"Yeah. Sometimes they do. Now my mom worries about our *losing* money."

Miss Eells shook her head. "Oh, no!"

Anthony grinned. "Yeah, but I don't worry on account of I don't listen to them any more. Whenever I hear them starting in to argue, I get up and close the door of my room. Then I can't hear them at all, and I go right to sleep."

Miss Eells laughed when she heard this.

Anthony studied another Assyrian relief for a moment, then he turned and asked earnestly, "Miss Eells, would you consider me to be a fool?"

Miss Eells's mouth dropped open. "Why, Tony, of course not. Why on earth do you ask?"

Anthony frowned. "Well," he said thoughtfully, "you know that old saying—'A fool and his money are soon parted' . . ."

Miss Eells laughed again. She laughed so loudly that a guard came up and told her to please be more quiet. Miss Eells said she was sorry. Then she looked at her watch and told Anthony that they had better go if they were going to catch the afternoon performance of the Chicago Symphony.

They walked out into the sunlight and started up the street toward the train.

ABOUT THE AUTHOR

John Bellairs is well-known for his gothic thrillers for young readers. He is the author of *THE HOUSE WITH A CLOCK IN ITS WALLS; THE FIGURE IN THE SHADOWS; THE LETTER, THE WITCH, AND THE RING; THE CURSE OF THE BLUE FIGURINE; THE MUMMY, THE WILL AND THE CRYPT; THE SPELL OF THE SORCERER'S SKULL;* and *THE DARK SECRET OF WEATHEREND,* which is a sequel to *THE TREASURE OF ALPHEUS WINTERBORN;* and *THE REVENGE OF THE WIZARD'S GHOST.* The first two titles were chosen by *THE NEW YORK TIMES* as Outstanding Books of the Year. He has also written several adult books, among them *THE FACE IN THE FROST* and *THE PEDANT AND THE SHUFFLY.*

Mr. Bellairs grew up in Michigan and lives in Haverhill, Massachusetts, where he is currently working on another scary book.

FROM THE SPOOKY, EERIE PEN OF JOHN BELLAIRS . . .

☐ **THE CURSE OF THE BLUE FIGURINE**   15429/$2.75

Johnny Dixon knows a lot about ancient Egypt and curses and evil spirits—but when he finds the blue figurine, he actually "sees" a frightening, super-natural world. Even his friend Professor Childermass can't help him!

☐ **THE MUMMY, THE WILL AND THE CRYPT**   15323/$2.50

For months Johnny has been working on a riddle that would lead to a $10,000 reward. Feeling certain that the money is hidden somewhere in the house of a dead man, Johnny goes into his house where a bolt of lightening reveals to him that the house is not quite deserted . . .

☐ **THE SPELL OF THE SORCERER'S SKULL**   15357/$2.50

Johnny Dixon is back, but this time he's not teamed up with Dr. Childermass. That's because his friend, the Professor, has disappeared!

☐ THE OWLSTONE CROWN

15349-8/$2.50

by X. J. Kennedy
When Timothy and Verity Tibbs follow a tiny ladybug private eye over a moon-lit path to Other Earth, magical adventures happen fast.

☐ BONES ON BLACK SPRUCE MOUNTAIN

15443/$2.25

by David Budbill
Thirteen-year-olds Danny and Seth set out to explore Black Spruce Mountain because they love camping out. But Black Spruce Mountain appears to be haunted and their adventure is more than they bargained for.

☐ SNOWSHOE TREK TO OTTER RIVER

15252/$1.95

by David Budbill
David and Seth have a lot in common besides their age. They share a love of adventure and specifically, they share a love of camping and exploring. And what better place to explore than the backwoods of Vermont?

☐ CHRISTOPHER

15363/$2.25

by Richard M. Koff
On a dare from a friend, Christopher knocks on the door of a haunted house. There he meets the "Headmaster" who teaches him how to release the amazing powers of his own mind.

JIM KJELGAARD

In these adventure stories, Jim Kjelgaard shows us the special world of animals, the wilderness, and the bonds between men and dogs. *Irish Red* and *Outlaw Red* are stories about two champion Irish setters. *Snow Dog* shows what happens when a half-wild dog crosses paths with a trapper. The cougar-hunting *Lion Hound* and the greyhound story *Desert Dog* take place in our present-day Southwest. And, *Stormy* is an extraordinary story of a boy and his devoted dog. You'll want to read all these exciting books.

☐	15456	A NOSE FOR TROUBLE	$2.50
☐	15368	HAUNT FOX	$2.25
☐	15434	BIG RED	$2.95
☐	15324	DESERT DOG	$2.50
☐	15286	IRISH RED: SON OF BIG RED	$2.50
☐	15427	LION HOUND	$2.95
☐	15339	OUTLAW RED	$2.50
☐	15365	SNOW DOG	$2.50
☐	15388	STORMY	$2.50
☐	15466	WILD TREK	$2.75

Prices and availability subject to change without notice.